*The burning hot water hit his lower lip.*

"Hey, cut it out!" Matt started to kick as hard as he could, but the hands stayed around his ankles, pulling him into the hot tub.

Another tug.

"*Help!*" he screamed. The water had turned scalding, and the hands pulled him down until his chin touched the surface.

"Stop!"

Another tug. The burning hot water hit his lower lip. Matt started splashing frantically.

"Help!" he cried. "Let me go!"

Another tug.

The water went over his mouth. Matt craned his neck to keep his nose out of the water as he struggled to take one more breath.

Another tug. A moment later, he disappeared under the bubbles.

Read these other thrillers
available from HarperPaperbacks

*Sweet Dreams*
*Sweetheart*
by Kate Daniel

*Class Trip*
by Bebe Faas Rice

*Deadly Stranger*
by M. C. Sumner

# NIGHTMARE INN

## T. S. Rue

HarperPaperbacks
*A Division of* HarperCollins*Publishers*

This is a work of fiction. The characters, incidents, and dialogues are products of the author's imagination and are not to be construed as real. Any resemblance to actual events or persons, living or dead, is entirely coincidental.

HarperPaperbacks *A Division of* HarperCollins*Publishers*
10 East 53rd Street, New York, N.Y. 10022



Produced by Daniel Weiss Associates, Inc.,
33 West 17th Street, New York, New York 10011.

First printing: March, 1993

Printed in the United States of America

HarperPaperbacks and colophon are trademarks of HarperCollins*Publishers*

10 9 8 7 6 5 4 3 2 1

# Chapter 1

"I can't believe my parents finally agreed to let me do this," Jodie Collins said. She sat down on the bed and pulled a pink brush through her long, straight black hair.

Across the room, Sarah Wilkins was staring into her dresser drawer, in the midst of some last-minute packing. But her thoughts were a million miles away from clothes at that moment.

"Sarah?" Jodie said.

"Huh?" Sarah looked up, surprised.

"Didn't you hear what I said?"

Sarah shook her head. She knew Jodie had said something, but she honestly couldn't remember. "What, Ellen?"

Jodie stared at her with a bewildered look on her face. "Ellen?" she asked. "Who's Ellen?"

Sarah stared back at her. She had no idea who Ellen was or why she'd mistakenly called Jodie by that name. She didn't even know anyone named Ellen. But ever since the night before, her thoughts had been totally scrambled.

"What planet are you on tonight?" Jodie asked.

"Earth, I think," Sarah said, uncomfortably. But it wasn't surprising that Jodie had noticed something was wrong. Sarah just didn't feel like herself. She'd been trying to avoid talking to Jodie all evening. It wasn't easy when you were in the same room together, and about to go away on a week-long trip with your boyfriends.

Fortunately, Jodie didn't seem to dwell on Sarah's spaciness. "I was just saying how I can't believe my parents are letting me go away with Adam for a week," she said, sweeping a loose black hair off her red plaid shirt. "Maybe they're getting Alzheimer's disease, or something."

When Sarah had first met her, she'd found Jodie's cynical, sarcastic sense of humor a little intimidating. But she'd gradually gotten used to it.

"Why?" Sarah asked, as she lifted a navy-blue sweatshirt out of her drawer and held it up against herself in the mirror. She liked the way navy contrasted with her curly, bright-red hair. "Don't they trust you?"

"I guess," Jodie said. Then she smiled. "I'm just not sure I trust myself."

Sarah quickly put down the sweatshirt and looked back into the drawer, hoping Jodie wouldn't notice how shaken she was. Sarah had grave doubts that she could trust herself, too.

"How about your parents?" Jodie asked.

"My parents?" Sarah went blank for a moment.

Jodie stared at her and rolled her eyes. "Yes, those two older people who share the bedroom across the hall and pay for all your clothes."

"Oh, uh, they don't have a problem with it," Sarah answered. The truth was, they hadn't seemed to care much one way or the other if she went away with Matt. They were both so preoccupied with their own lives that they rarely had an opinion about hers. Too bad for her, because at this moment, Sarah would give anything to get out of this trip. She wished they had just said no.

"You told them you were going away with Matt and another couple to a secluded cabin in the woods for a week, and they just said 'fine'?" Jodie asked.

"Basically," Sarah said. She put down the navy sweatshirt and picked up a red one. "I told them the cabin had separate bedrooms, and we'd stay in one and the boys would stay in the other."

"Wow. I practically had to beg my parents for a month," Jodie said. "I never thought they'd let me go away with Adam."

At the sound of Jodie's boyfriend's name, Sarah cringed.

"Why didn't your parents give you a hard time?" Jodie asked.

"They said if I was going to do anything wrong, it would be just as easy for me to do it around here as way out in the woods somewhere."

What had happened to Sarah the night before had certainly proved that to be true.

"Amazing," Jodie said. "Imagine anyone's parents being that rational. Maybe that's the way people from Middleburg are."

"It's Middletown," Sarah corrected her. "And I think they're the same as people anywhere else."

Sarah's family had moved from Middletown to Glendale that past summer. She and Jodie weren't exactly friends, but they spent a lot of time together because their boyfriends, Matt and Adam, were best friends.

"Well," Jodie said. "It seems to me that you're pretty levelheaded."

Her words sent a shiver through Sarah. *If only Jodie knew the truth.*

A few moments later, a car horn blew outside. Sarah recognized it as Matt's parents' Isuzu, which they were lending to Matt for the trip. Across the room, Jodie pulled the brush through her hair one last time, and then put it in the zipper pocket of her dark-green backpack.

"Matt's here," she said, jumping off the bed and picking up the pack.

Sarah was still staring into the drawer, unable to decide which sweatshirt to take. But she knew what the basis for her indecision really was. It was her dread of going away on this trip. If only some miracle would occur that would prevent it from happening. An earthquake or something . . .

"Hey, come on." Jodie stopped in the doorway. "What are you waiting for?"

Sarah held up both sweatshirts. "I just can't decide which one to take."

Jodie marched back to Sarah, took both sweatshirts out of her hands, and stuffed them into Sarah's blue backpack. "Take them both."

"Then my backpack will be too heavy," Sarah complained.

"That's what Matt's for," Jodie said, pulling her by the hand.

"Huh?"

"To carry your pack when it gets too heavy," Jodie explained, impatiently. "Wow, you really are out of it tonight. Now, come on, before someone's parents figure out that they're crazy to be letting us do this."

Sarah picked up her pack and followed Jodie down the stairs and through the living room, where her father sat on the couch watching golf on the television and eating popcorn from a large yellow bowl. He probably wouldn't even have noticed that Sarah was leaving, if she hadn't said "good-bye."

"Have a good trip," he said, and waved without taking his eyes from the television.

Sarah and Jodie were practically to the front door when Mrs. Wilkins stuck her head out of the den, where she'd been busy working with her computer.

"Oh, wait, honey," she called.

Jodie and Sarah gave each other a look.

"What, Mom?" Sarah asked, praying her mother had suddenly changed her mind and decided she shouldn't go.

"Did you remember to take my dirty clothes to the dry cleaners today?" Mrs. Wilkins asked.

"Yes, Mom," Sarah said, with a sigh. "I left the laundry ticket on your bureau."

"And you left your room neat?"

"Yes, Mom."

"Okay, have a good trip," Mrs. Wilkins said.

"Thanks, Mom," Sarah said, opening the front door. The incredible thing was, neither her mother nor father had bothered to ask exactly where she was going.

Outside, the April evening air was cool and crisp. Sarah took a deep breath and stared up at the reddish-orange sun as it set in the cloudless blue sky. She looked down the street, but there was no sign of Matt or his car.

"I could have sworn I heard him honk," Jodie said, walking down to the curb. "Didn't you?"

Sarah nodded. She'd heard the Isuzu's horn too. But she wasn't completely surprised that the car was nowhere in sight—not when Matt was involved.

"Is this another one of Matt's stupid jokes?" Jodie asked.

"What do you think?" Sarah replied.

A moment later, the white Isuzu Trooper came around the corner. As it rolled toward them, Jodie suddenly gasped. "There's no one driving!"

It was true. The driver's seat was empty. The car seemed to be driving itself. And it was headed right toward Sarah and Jodie.

"Run!" Jodie shouted.

# Chapter 2

Jodie dropped her pack and dashed up the driveway toward the house. Sarah glanced at the house, but remained at the curb—right in the car's path.

The Isuzu was headed directly at her. . . .

"Look out, Sarah!" Jodie shouted.

But Sarah didn't move. When the Trooper was less than five feet away, it suddenly skidded to a stop. Sarah just smiled and stared at the empty driver's seat. The engine roared menacingly, as if the car was going to charge forward. Still, Sarah didn't budge.

"Very funny, Matt," she yelled over the roar of the engine.

The engine revved loudly again.

"Okay, Matt," Sarah shouted. "It's not funny anymore."

A second later, Matt's disheveled sandy-colored

hair appeared over the dashboard, and he stared at her with a disappointed look on his face.

"How'd you know?" he asked, brushing the hair out of his eyes.

"Matt, if it had been anyone else in the world, I wouldn't have known," Sarah said, walking around to the driver's side window, where Jodie joined them. "But with you, I always know."

"Where were you?" Jodie asked.

"Lying on the floor," Matt said.

"I can't believe you'd drive without being able to see where you were going," Jodie said in amazement.

"He could see," Sarah said, reaching in through the open window and taking out a paper periscope with mirrors in it. It was just like the one her father took to golf tournaments so he could see over the crowds.

"Well, I thought it was a pretty good trick," Matt said to Sarah. "I guess you're too smart for me."

The words stung. Matt was usually good-natured, but there was an anger in his voice that Sarah had never heard before.

Matt pulled the car into the driveway and got out. He was wearing a pair of worn jeans with dirt and grass stains on the knees. His tan chamois shirt was wrinkled, and the laces of his hiking boots were undone and hung loosely to the ground. When he saw their packs, he stopped and ran his fingers through his sandy-colored hair again.

"Okay, I'd better take care of these first," he said, opening the Isuzu's rear door. He grabbed Jodie's pack and lifted it into the back. Then he reached for Sarah's.

"Hey, what did you pack in here?" he asked, sounding a little grouchy. "Rocks?"

Sarah was immediately on guard. Was he grouchy because he somehow knew what had happened the night before? It didn't seem possible.

Unless Adam had told him . . .

"I, uh, couldn't decide what to take," she said, cautiously watching him.

"I know, so you took everything," Matt said as he shut the rear door. "That's one thing about Jodie. She always travels light."

Sarah felt a slight chill. She hated it when Matt compared her to Jodie. But she figured it was unavoidable, considering Matt and Jodie's history together. Jodie and Matt had gone together all through junior high, and even after they broke up, they stayed good friends. After what had happened the night before, Sarah wasn't certain she had a right to let anything that had occurred between Matt and Jodie bother her.

Matt got back into the driver's seat, and the girls got in on the passenger side, with Sarah sitting in the front next to Matt, and Jodie sitting on the bench seat in back.

"Okay, let's get this show on the road," Matt

said, slapping his hands together. A moment later, he pulled the Trooper out of the Wilkinses' driveway. Sarah gazed out the passenger window, unable to look at Matt without feeling a great pang of guilt and regret.

"As long as we don't forget you-know-who," Jodie said from the backseat.

"My best bud?" Matt said, as he put the Isuzu into forward gear and accelerated down the street. "No way. We're headed there right now."

The thought that she would be seeing Adam again in a few moments filled Sarah with dread. She even considered pretending to have a stomachache, but Matt would probably just stop at the drugstore and get her something for it. Meanwhile, Matt stopped the car at a light, and began fiddling with the radio dial.

Then suddenly, he turned to her.

"What happened to you last night?" he asked, staring intensely into her eyes.

Sarah looked away. "I . . . I went to the mall to get some long underwear," she stammered.

"Yeah, but I called at ten thirty, a good hour after the mall closed," Matt said. "And your mother said you still hadn't come home."

"That's funny," Jodie said from the backseat. "I called Adam last night around the same time, and he wasn't home either."

Sarah said nothing. The light turned green. As Matt pressed on the gas pedal, he looked at

Jodie in the rearview mirror. "You don't think they were fooling around behind our backs, do you?" he asked.

"Matt!" Sarah gasped.

"Hey, I was just kidding," Matt said. But he didn't smile.

# Chapter 3

A few minutes later, the Isuzu rolled into Adam's driveway. Matt turned to Sarah and Jodie. "You guys want to help Adam bring the stuff out?" he asked. "I'll make room in the back."

Instead of getting out, Jodie reached forward and turned the radio from music to a news station.

"Go ahead," she said. "I'm going to listen to the weather report."

The last thing Sarah wanted to do was go into Adam's house alone, but she knew if she refused it might seem strange, so she got out and slowly went up the slate walk. Through the glass storm door, she could see that the front door was open. Lying in the hallway were a backpack, some sleeping bags, and fishing rods.

Adam was nowhere in sight.

Sarah pushed open the storm door, hoping she could grab a couple of sleeping bags and head back to the car without running into him. She bent down and picked up two sleeping bags, then rose and turned. Suddenly, she gasped.

Adam was standing right behind her. She hadn't even heard him come up. He was staring at her with his dark-blue eyes, a tuft of his brown hair curling down onto his forehead. Sarah tore her eyes away from his, wishing he weren't so handsome.

"I'm glad you came in alone," he said quietly, glancing out the door.

"Why?" Sarah asked, taking a step back.

"Wait." Adam reached toward her, then realized what he was doing and let his arm drop. "I just wanted to talk to you about last night."

"What about it?" Sarah asked nervously.

"Well, you know, about what happened."

Sarah glanced back out through the storm door, terrified that Matt or Jodie would see them. "I'm sorry, Doug, but I can't talk about it now."

Adam looked perplexed. "Why are you calling me Doug? Who's Doug?"

Instead of answering, Sarah turned and went quickly outside with the sleeping bags. She had no idea who Doug was, or why she'd called Adam by that name. But it was the second time in less than an hour that she'd called someone she knew well by the wrong name. Normally she never did things like that. Could it have been because of what happened the night before? Or was there something else going on?

"Has he got much more stuff than this?" Matt asked as Sarah handed him the sleeping bags and he threw them in the back of the car. As was Matt's style, everything was piled up haphazardly.

"Not that much," Sarah said. "I think he can bring the rest out himself." She climbed into the front seat of the Trooper. Jodie was still sitting in the backseat. The radio was playing music again.

"Think we've got everything?" she asked.

"As soon as Matt throws it all in," Sarah said.

"He just hates to organize anything," Jodie said.

It always made Sarah uncomfortable when Jodie spoke in such familiar terms about Matt, but she knew Jodie couldn't help it.

That past summer, soon after Sarah and her family had moved to Glendale, she had met Matt at the town pool and had started going out with him. Matt always had a lot to say about Adam, and had spoken of him in very admiring tones, but he'd hardly said anything all summer to Sarah about Jodie. Then the summer ended, and Jodie and Adam came home from their summer jobs as camp counselors. Suddenly the four of them were going on double dates almost every weekend, and Sarah couldn't help feeling a little jealous and suspicious of the former boyfriend and girlfriend.

Now Sarah wondered what Matt would say if he knew that the previous night Sarah had found herself in his best friend's arms.

Sarah heard the front door to Adam's house close as he came out carrying his backpack and the fishing rods. Unlike Matt, he was dressed neatly in khakis and a heavy denim shirt.

"I can't believe he really thinks we're going to eat the fish they catch," Jodie whispered, watching Adam and Matt load the last of the gear. "I mean, do you even like camping?"

"Actually, I've sort of been looking forward to it," Sarah said. *At least, I was until last night.*

"Why?" Jodie asked.

"Because it's something I never get to do," Sarah said. "My parents' idea of an adventure is trying a new restaurant."

"Talk about restaurants," Jodie said. "Did you bring the freeze-dried food?"

Sarah nodded. "Enough scrambled eggs and corned-beef hash to last a week. That's one of the reasons my pack weighs so much. What did you bring?"

"Only essentials, like mint-chocolate Girl Scout cookies, Mallomars, and Fig Newtons."

Outside the car, Adam stopped and stared. "You call this packed, Matt?" he asked, gesturing at the gear piled helter-skelter in the back.

"Sure," Matt replied with a shrug. "What's wrong?"

Instead of being critical, Adam just smiled. "Nothing. Just give me a couple of minutes."

They waited while Adam neatly repacked the

gear. Sarah couldn't help thinking how different Matt and Adam were. Although he never smelled, or anything gross like that, Matt always looked really sloppy. Adam, on the other hand, was always neat. Sarah hated to admit it, but she preferred neatness to sloppiness.

The rear door slammed. A second later, Matt got in the front, and Adam got in the back next to Jodie.

"Hey, good-looking," Adam said with a smile, and kissed Jodie quickly. In the front, Sarah watched them out of the corner of her eye, feeling uncomfortable. She wished he wouldn't do that.

"Okay," Matt said, turning the key. "This is your last chance. Does everybody have everything they need?"

"I forgot my hair dryer," Jodie said.

"You won't need it," Adam said. "My uncle's cabin doesn't have electricity."

"You never told me that," Jodie gasped.

"What's the big deal?" Adam asked.

"The big deal is, I have to finish reading *David Copperfield* on this trip," Jodie said. "I have to do a report on it when I get back."

"No problem," Adam said. "You'll be able to read by the Coleman lantern."

Jodie sighed. "When you said we were going to rough it, I had no idea you meant *that* rough."

"I guarantee, you'll love it," Adam said.

"Okay," Matt said. "Now, does everyone have what they need? This is really your last chance."

The thing Sarah needed most was to get away and try to understand what had happened the night before. But it was the one thing she couldn't ask for. As Matt started to back the Isuzu out of Adam's driveway, she sighed and slumped down in her seat. This was going to be the longest week of her life.

# Chapter 4

The first three hours of the drive passed quickly. They listened to tapes and talked about the track meet held the previous day. Sarah was a runner. She loved to run, and had been doing it ever since she was little. The day before, she'd finished first in the mile, and second in the four-forty.

"Isn't there a meet against Burns right after we get back?" Matt asked.

"Yes," Sarah said.

"How are you going to stay in shape for it?" Matt asked.

"He's right," Adam said. "I hate to tell you this, but you won't find any tracks to practice on where we're going."

Every time Sarah heard Adam's voice, she felt something stir inside her. They both knew what they were hiding. They both knew they were pretending.

*If only Matt and Jodie weren't here.*

"That's okay," Sarah replied, trying to sound normal. "When I was a kid I used to run through the woods."

What she didn't say was that she hoped to spend *a lot* of time in the woods. Anything to stay away from Matt and Jodie.

Matt maintained a steady sixty-five miles per hour on the dark highway. After a while, Adam told him which exit to get off on, and they turned onto a two-lane road that seemed to grow narrower as they got deeper and deeper into the forest. Soon all they could see in the headlights were the dark shadows of the trees lining both sides of the road. The moon had completely disappeared from view.

"Hey, this is pretty spooky," Matt said.

"It's unspoiled forestland," Adam said. "The way the world used to be, before man came along and paved everything over."

"Well, I wouldn't mind if he'd just come along and added some streetlights and a McDonald's," Jodie said, staring uncomfortably out the window.

"You don't need streetlights," Adam said. "Out here you've got the stars and the moon."

Sarah looked out her window into the night sky, but she still couldn't see the moon, or a single star.

About a half hour after they'd turned off the

highway, raindrops began to hit the windshield. First a few random ones, then more and more, until Matt had to turn on the windshield wipers.

"Hey, I thought you said the forecast was for clear skies," Matt said, looking in the rearview mirror at Adam.

"That's what I heard," Adam said.

"I heard it too," Jodie said. "Just a couple of hours ago, at Adam's house. Clear and cool tonight, and sunny tomorrow. And the extended forecast said it would be that way for the rest of the week."

"Well, this isn't exactly what I call clear," Matt said, staring at the windshield.

Sarah turned toward Matt, but at the same time, she could see Adam out of the corner of her eye. "Do you think we should go back home and wait a day to see if it clears up?" she asked hopefully.

"Naw, this is probably just a freak storm," Adam said. "Besides, we're more than halfway there by now."

Sarah turned to face him. Adam stared right back at her, his face unreadable. The rain was a perfect excuse to delay the trip. Why didn't he want to? Why wasn't he as uncomfortable about this as she was?

Matt had to slow the Isuzu to a crawl as the rain continued to come down harder and harder. The road narrowed still more, with deep ditches on either side.

"It'll be real interesting if we meet a car coming the other way," Matt said, trying to peer through the windshield, as the rain was swished away by the wipers and the car bumped along on the rutted road.

"Don't worry, you'll see their headlights," Adam reassured him.

"It's not that," said Matt. "This road's so narrow, there's hardly room to pass. If someone comes from the other direction, one of us is going to wind up in the ditch." Sarah knew that tone of voice. Matt was trying not to sound nervous, but he was gripping the wheel so tightly she could see the skin on his knuckles turning white.

Suddenly Sarah lurched forward against her seat belt, as Matt slammed on the brakes and the Isuzu skidded to a stop.

"What happened?" Jodie gasped.

"Nothing," Matt said. "Sorry, I didn't mean to hit the brakes that hard. But look."

He pointed through the wet windshield. Ten yards ahead, the road ended, and the headlights illuminated a yellow sign with a double-headed arrow. Matt turned and looked back at Adam.

"Which way?" Matt asked.

Adam bit his lip. "I don't remember this. I wonder if we missed a turn somewhere back there."

"I didn't see any other roads," Matt said.

The pouring rain pummeled the roof of the car. Inside, everyone was quiet.

"Maybe we ought to turn back," Sarah said, breaking the silence.

"It's a long way," Matt said.

"I'm sure we took the right exit off the highway," Adam said. "Try making a right. If it's wrong, we'll just turn around."

Matt started to make a right turn. As they passed close to the double-headed sign, Sarah saw that, instead of being held up by a signpost, it was nailed to a large old tree with gnarled and bent branches. It was strange, but she could have sworn she'd seen that sign and that tree once before.

But when?

# Chapter 5

They followed the road for several miles in silence, as Matt steered around large potholes and fallen branches. The rain continued to pour down, and an occasional bolt of lightning sliced through the pitch-black sky. During these bursts of light, Sarah could see that there was nothing but dark forest on either side of them. Now, fog began to mix with the heavy rain, and Matt flicked on the special fog lights mounted on the Isuzu's bumper. They all peered anxiously out the windshield, looking for signs.

"Does any of this look familiar?" Matt asked as he wrestled with the steering wheel, guiding the Isuzu around the obstacles in the road.

"No, but . . . Oh, yeah! Look!" Adam pointed.

They stared outside at the dark, wet tree trunks.

"Look at what?" Matt asked.

"See that 'No Trespassing' sign?" Adam asked.

Sarah squinted ahead. Nailed to a tree trunk near the side of the road was a white paper sign warning that trespassers would be shot.

"What about it?" Matt asked.

"I remember seeing one like it on the way to my uncle's place," Adam said.

"Give me a break," Matt said. "It's just a standard sign. I've seen a hundred of them."

"Yeah, but the tree looks familiar, too," Adam said.

"Great," Matt mumbled. He kept on going. "I think I've seen a few hundred of those, too."

Another hour passed. By now, it was past midnight. The narrow, potholed road just seemed to wind on forever through the fog. Despite the deep sense of anxiety they all shared, Sarah felt herself growing tired. She'd hardly gotten any sleep the previous night, and her eyelids were starting to grow heavy.

Then once again, she felt the Isuzu stop.

"Now what?" Jodie asked.

"Take a look," Matt said.

Through the rain and fog they could see that the broken and crumbling pavement had ended. Ahead of them was a muddy, rutted dirt road.

"All right!" Adam said.

"What's all right about it?" Jodie asked.

"I remember the road to my uncle's place goes from asphalt to dirt just before you get there,"

Adam said. "I bet the cabin is just ahead."

Sarah felt her heart sink. All hopes for them turning around and abandoning this trip now seemed to be lost.

"Good thing we've got four-wheel drive," Matt said, shifting the gear lever.

With a lurch, the Isuzu started forward again. For a while, they bounced and skidded along the muddy road. Adam kept saying he was certain they'd come to the cabin soon. All Sarah knew was that the rocking and sliding seemed to be making her more and more drowsy until she could hardly keep her eyes open.

Suddenly there was something dark in the road ahead of them. It was growing larger. Sarah blinked. Another vehicle was coming toward them! As it grew in the headlights of the Isuzu, Sarah saw that it looked like a big old school bus with its headlights off. A split second elapsed as Sarah waited for Matt to pull off to the right and let the bus pass, but Matt just kept driving right down the middle of the muddy road as if nothing was there. Now the school bus was only about thirty feet away!

"Look out!" Sarah cried.

Matt bent forward and stared ahead. "For what?"

There was no time to explain. The bus was about to hit them.

Why couldn't Matt see it?

Sarah had no time to find out. She wanted to

avoid a head-on collision. She quickly reached over and grabbed the wheel and yanked it, sending the Isuzu veering to the right and just narrowly avoiding a crash with the bus.

In the back, Jodie screamed as the Isuzu's front end tipped downward into a ditch, and the car jolted to a sudden stop. Sarah was thrown forward, and she felt the shoulder strap of the seat belt snap tight across her chest. She stared out the window as the old school bus hurtled past, its side covered with strange flowery decorations and peace signs.

It appeared to be painted pink.

"Is everybody okay?" Adam asked quickly.

Sarah and the others nodded.

"Jeez, what was that all about?" Matt was staring at her.

"You didn't see it?" Sarah asked in amazement.

"See what?"

"That . . . that school bus."

Matt frowned and looked back at Jodie and Adam. "Anyone see a school bus?"

Jodie and Adam shook their heads.

Matt turned back to Sarah. "I think I would have known if a school bus had been coming toward us," he said. "They're kind of hard to miss."

"It was all pink, and covered with decorations," Sarah said. "Like something from Woodstock."

"I think you were dreaming," Matt said.

"No, Matt, I swear I saw it," Sarah insisted. "It was headed right for us. We're lucky we weren't crushed."

"By a *pink* school bus?" Matt looked doubtful.

Sarah became aware of how crazy it sounded. But she was certain she'd seen it, wasn't she? Or was Matt right? Could it possibly have been a dream?

No one else said anything, and for a few seconds Sarah listened to the rain pelting the car roof. Because the front end of the car was tilted down into the ditch, Sarah felt the shoulder strap of her seat belt digging against her shoulder and chest. The pressure was making it difficult for her to breathe.

"Okay, let's forget it," Adam said. "Let's get back on the road. We can't be too far from my uncle's place now."

Matt put the Isuzu in reverse and hit the gas. They heard the high-pitched whine as the tires spun through the mud.

"Darn, we're stuck," he muttered.

Sarah gasped for air while Matt repeatedly jammed the car into forward and then into reverse, trying to rock it out of the ditch.

The Isuzu hardly budged.

"Any other ideas?" Matt asked.

Sarah shook her head, finally catching her breath. Once again, Matt tried rocking the car out of the mud.

But it was hopeless. Finally he gave up and pressed his forehead against the steering wheel.

"Great," he muttered. "Now we're not going anywhere."

# Chapter 6

The wind had picked up, swirling the rain around the car. Sarah watched little rivulets run down the windows. Outside, in the headlight beams, all they could see were the dark, bare trunks and branches of trees and the ghostly fog drifting through them.

"I thought this car had four-wheel drive," Jodie said.

"It does," Matt replied. "But there are some things even four-wheel drive can't get you out of. Like a muddy ditch."

"So, what do we do?" Sarah asked.

Matt gave her a look. She could see that he still blamed her for pulling the car off the road. But she couldn't have helped it. For that one instant, that school bus had been as real as the nose on her face.

"I guess we sit and wait for someone to come by and help us," Jodie said.

Matt gazed out the window. "I really doubt anyone's going to come by on this road at this time of night. . . . Except maybe another pink school bus."

Sarah felt her cheeks burn. It wasn't fair. *They're all blaming me*, she thought. It wasn't right, but she was worried. First she'd started calling them by the wrong names. Then she'd seen that school bus the others swore wasn't there. She never did things like that.

"Look, I'm certain the cabin wasn't that far from where the paved road ended," Adam said. "Maybe we should try walking the rest of the way."

"In the rain and dark?" Jodie asked.

"I brought a waterproof flashlight," Adam said. "Our rain gear will keep us dry."

"What rain gear?" Matt asked.

"Didn't you guys bring any?" Adam asked.

The others shook their heads slowly.

"The weather report said 'no rain,'" Jodie explained.

"Well, I brought a rain jacket," Adam said. "And I have an old poncho I was going to use as a ground tarp. The girls could wear them. At least they'll stay dry."

Even in this difficult situation, Sarah couldn't help noticing how thoughtful and considerate Adam was. Matt had never been like that.

"Meanwhile, you and I will get soaked," Matt said to Adam.

"Yeah, for a while," Adam said. "Then we'll dry off."

"We could stay in here and tell ghost stories," Matt said.

"*No!*" Sarah heard herself suddenly cry.

The others turned and looked at her, puzzled. Sarah herself couldn't understand why she'd reacted so strongly. "Even walking in the rain sounds better than that," she said quickly.

"What do you think, girls?" Adam said. "Should we go for it?"

Sarah met Jodie's questioning gaze, and then turned away to look out the window at the dark fog and rain. The last thing she wanted to do was go out there. But staying in the car all night posed other problems. If they stayed, they'd talk. And sooner or later, the talk would turn again to wondering where Sarah and Adam had been the previous night. She looked back at Jodie.

"I think we should try it," Sarah said.

Jodie looked surprised.

"Then it's agreed," Adam said. "We'll just take our packs for now. We can come back to get the car and the rest of the gear in the morning."

The girls watched as Matt and Adam pushed open their doors and got out. Suddenly the roar of the rain was much louder, and a cold damp mist floated into the car. The boys went around to the rear to get the packs. Jodie turned to Sarah.

"I can't believe you want to walk through

this," she said in a low voice, so the boys wouldn't hear.

"I thought it would be better than sitting in here all night," Sarah whispered.

"Well, I hope you made the right decision," Jodie said.

"So do I," Sarah replied.

A few minutes later, they were walking single file along the dark, muddy road, with Adam and his waterproof flashlight in the lead. Sarah walked behind Adam, wearing the old olive-green poncho, her shoes sticking in the wet mud with each step. The rain sounded like kernels of corn popping as it pelted her hood.

"How much farther, Adam?" Jodie asked, as she slogged along through the mud behind Sarah. She was wearing a yellow rain jacket. Matt brought up the rear, his chamois shirt soaked through.

"Not too much . . . I think."

Sarah heard the uncertainty in his voice. It frightened her, but at least she was relatively dry and comfortable. The only problem was the rain-water dripping off the hood of the poncho, rolling down her forehead and tickling the tip of her nose. She was walking with her head down in order to stop the drops from hitting her face.

Suddenly she bumped into something.

"Hey!" Adam said.

Sarah realized she'd bumped into his back. He'd stopped for some reason. She looked up and followed the beam of the flashlight through the mist and rain to a point ahead where the road forked. A huge, scraggly, bare-limbed tree stood at the beginning of the fork.

"*The Arcadia*," Sarah said.

"What?" Adam asked, staring at her.

"Uh . . ." Sarah didn't know what to say. Why had she said that? What was the Arcadia? "Nothing."

"Did you say something about an arcade?" Jodie asked, as she came up behind them.

"Sounded more like Arcadia to me," Adam said.

"What is that?" Matt asked.

All Sarah could do was shrug. "I don't know. It was just something that popped into my head."

The others stared at her for a moment more. Then Matt shrugged. "Well, at least it wasn't another school bus."

Sarah watched as Adam, Matt, and Jodie looked around in the pouring rain.

"You remember this?" Jodie asked Adam.

The rain had slicked Adam's hair down. He slowly shook his head. "No, not really."

"Oh, great," Matt said. "Now what?"

"We'd better go back to the car," Jodie said, nervously. "It's crazy to just wander around in the pouring rain all night."

But Adam stepped toward the old tree and aimed the flashlight around the brush and brambles that surrounded it.

"Hey, look at this!" he called, stepping into the brush and lifting something up.

The others moved forward as Adam pulled up an old wooden sign that must have fallen down years ago. Sarah felt a chill. With the flashlight shining on the sign, they were just able to make out an arrow pointing toward the left-hand fork, and the words: *The Arcadia Inn.*

Suddenly, Sarah was blinded by the glare of Adam's flashlight shining in her eyes.

# Chapter 7

"How did you know?" Adam asked.

Sarah held her hand up to shield her eyes. "You're blinding me."

Adam lowered the flashlight. Lightning flashed above, and a crash of thunder made them jump. Sarah looked down and saw that the rainwater was now rushing by her feet like a small river. She knew they were waiting for an answer, but she didn't have one. She'd never heard of the Arcadia before. It wasn't possible that her parents had taken her there. Her parents never took her anywhere.

"So?" Adam asked.

"I don't know," was all Sarah could say.

"You have to know," Adam insisted. "You couldn't have made it up."

"I swear, I don't know," Sarah said.

"You think we could worry about this later?"

Jodie asked. "I mean, I'd really like to get out of the rain."

Adam just stared at Sarah without talking. She could see he was really puzzled. But so was she.

"What do we do now?" Matt asked.

"Well, the sign said that the Arcadia Inn is that way," Adam said, pointing toward the left-hand fork.

"But it's an old sign," Jodie said.

"Maybe we could find someone and get help," Adam said.

"If the Arcadia is in the same condition as this sign, I doubt it's worth going there. The place is probably deserted," Matt said.

"But it might be okay, or there might be some other place," Adam said. "I think we should take a look."

"What do you think?" Jodie asked Sarah.

Sarah was still wondering how she knew about that sign. She was certain she'd never heard the name before in her life. Why were all these weird things happening?

"Sarah?"

"Huh?"

"I asked what you thought," Jodie said.

"About what?"

Jodie shook her head. "Boy, you really are out of it."

Suddenly a strong gust of wind rattled the tree branches. The group put their hands over their faces to protect their eyes.

"Maybe Adam's right," Matt said. "I almost don't care where we go, as long as it's dry and I can change out of these wet clothes. Even my underwear's soaked."

"Well, I guess we should go check out the Arcadia Inn," Adam said. "Whatever it is." The next thing they knew, he'd started down the left-hand fork.

It seemed as though they walked forever. They came to more forks, made more guesses, and took more turns. Each time, Adam argued that it made sense to continue forward rather than go back. Sarah's legs grew tired, and her shoulders hurt from the straps of the backpack. After trudging through the mud and hundreds of puddles, the water had seeped through her hiking boots, making her socks feel squishy. But none of those sensations was as bad as the sensation of being lost at night, in the rain, deep in the woods, hundreds of miles from home.

"What the . . . ?" Ahead of them, Adam had stopped again. They all stood perfectly still, staring in amazement at a large white sign with gold carved letters welcoming them to *The New Arcadia*. Behind the sign, down a long paved driveway lined with neatly trimmed shrubs, was a large, old, white country inn. The windows were dark at that time of night, but smoke curled out of several tall brick chimneys.

"I must be dreaming," Jodie sighed.

"What is this place doing out here in the middle of nowhere?" Adam asked.

"Who cares?" Matt said. "Let's go get dry."

They started quickly down the driveway. Suddenly Matt stopped and looked back at Sarah, who was still standing near the sign, staring at the inn. "Hey, what are you waiting for?"

"Uh, nothing." Sarah started to follow them reluctantly. Something incredibly weird was going on. From the second she saw the inn, she felt certain that she'd been there before.

# Chapter 8

Sarah caught up with the others just in time to see Adam put his hand around the brass doorknob and try to turn it. "Darn, it's locked."

"Look." Jodie pointed at a button in the door frame. A small brass plaque above it said "Night Bell."

"Let's pray someone's here," Jodie said, pressing the button.

"We saw smoke from the chimneys," Matt said through chattering teeth. Sarah knew the boys, who were both soaked to the skin, must have been freezing in the cold rain. Her thoughts drifted back to the inn, and she stepped back and stared at the tall white colonial-style building again.

"Look familiar?" Adam suddenly asked, startling her.

Sarah quickly shook her head and looked back at the door.

They waited for a few moments, but no one came to the door.

Matt pushed the button next. "Come on," he muttered. "Let us in."

On the second floor, a light went on. Moments later, an outdoor light snapped on and they heard the click of a lock being turned.

The massive door swung open.

A man with long gray hair that fell past his shoulders stood before them. It was obvious that he'd hastily pulled on an old, patched denim shirt and jeans. His feet were bare, and his chin was covered with several days' worth of gray stubble. He wore half a dozen silver and turquoise rings, and a heavy silver and turquoise bracelet on his left wrist.

"We're really sorry to bother you," Adam said. "Our car got stuck in a ditch down the road, and we're trying to get some help."

The man shook his head. "Sorry, there's no one here who can pull a car out of a ditch at this time of night."

"Then maybe you could just give us a place to stay for the night," Jodie pleaded.

The man's gray eyes narrowed and the spidery wrinkles deepened as he looked from face to face. "I'd like to help, but we're not—" He stopped speaking as his eyes met Sarah's. For a moment, they just stared at each other, then Sarah looked away. She was certain she'd never seen him before, but still, there was an eerie, familiar feeling about him.

"Sure," the man said, holding the door open for them. "You can crash here for the night. We haven't opened for the season yet, but we keep a couple of the rooms made up for unexpected guests."

"Wow, thanks," Jodie said with a sigh of relief.

"Yeah, really," added Matt.

They stepped inside. The warm, dry air felt good, and Sarah was glad to get her heavy backpack off.

"Said your car went off the road?" the man asked, as he closed the door behind them.

"Yeah," Matt said, wiping the rainwater off his face. "Does anyone around here own an old pink school bus?"

The man studied him for a moment. "Why do you ask?"

Matt pointed at Sarah. "Because she thought she saw it coming at us with its headlights off. That's why we went off the road."

The man nodded slowly, his eyes on Sarah again. "Well, there used to be one around, but that was a long, long time ago."

A few minutes later, the gray-haired man led them through the spacious lobby and down a corridor lined with rooms. The inn was three stories high and had two wings that ran from either side of the central lobby. They passed an alcove with an ice chest, and soda and candy machines.

"You think we could use your phone to call for a tow truck?" Matt asked.

"It's too late now, but I'll call the garage for you in the morning," the man said.

"The car's probably a couple of miles up the road," Adam said.

"Okay."

"Tell them it's a white Isuzu," Matt said.

"A white what?" the man asked.

"Isuzu Trooper," Matt said. "You know, it's a four-wheel-drive vehicle."

"A Trooper." The man shook his head. "I guess things have changed. Used to be the only four-wheel-drive vehicles you saw around were Jeeps." He stopped partway down the hall and pointed at a door. "Why don't you girls stay here in room four. You boys can stay in room five, right across the hall. There are two twin beds per room, so you'll each have your own."

"Great," Adam said. "My father gave me his credit card just in case of emergencies. I'll be glad to pay."

"Don't worry about the bread, dude," the man said, glancing again at Sarah. "Get some sleep and enjoy your stay."

Then he turned and walked slowly away, leaving them standing in the dimly lit corridor. Sarah listened to his footsteps echoing off the walls as he disappeared from sight. She looked down the hall in the other direction. It seemed as if there was an endless line of identical doors.

"That guy was pretty weird," Matt whispered. "I mean, who uses words like 'crash' and 'bread' anymore? At least, when they mean sleeping and money?"

"He seemed nice enough to me," Adam said. "I'm just grateful he's letting us stay."

"Yeah, you're right," Matt said. He shivered. "I'm totally soaked. I can't wait to get dried off." He started to push open the door to room five, then turned back to them. "See you in the morning," he said, and disappeared inside.

Jodie turned and pushed open the door to room four.

"See you in the morning," Adam said.

"Just don't wake me too early," Jodie said with a yawn, and went in.

Suddenly Sarah and Adam were alone in the hall. Sarah felt goose bumps rise on her arms, but she knew it wasn't from the cold.

"How did you know about this place?" Adam asked.

"I don't know," Sarah replied. "I mean, I'm not sure that I did know about it."

"You knew the name," Adam said. "And I watched you while we waited outside. The way you were looking at the inn . . ."

Sarah felt his intense gaze on her. She was surprised to find that she wasn't shying away from it, the way she'd been earlier. Instead, she felt herself drawn to him. She actually had to fight the desire to step into his arms.

"Funny, how we keep winding up together," Adam said in a low voice.

Sarah's eyes widened. Was he feeling it too? Maybe what had happened the night before wasn't an accident. She took a step toward him, and then caught herself. What was she thinking? She was Matt's girlfriend, and Adam was with Jodie. Both of them were just a few feet away in their rooms. They might come back out at any second, and even if they didn't, this was still wrong. She quickly went into her room and shut the door.

"I think we're lucky," Jodie said. They were each in their own beds, lying in the dark.

"Why?" Sarah asked.

"I just bet this inn is a whole lot nicer than Adam's uncle's cabin." Jodie yawned. "Oh, well, I guess we'll see tomorrow. Good night."

In the dim light, Sarah watched Jodie turn over and pull her blanket up to her shoulder. Despite the fact that she'd barely slept the night before and had been dozing in the car, Sarah felt wide awake. So many strange things had happened. Calling her friends by the wrong names, knowing about the Arcadia, the way that strange man with the long gray hair had acted toward her, and then her feelings about Adam, which suddenly felt so intense . . .

How was she ever going to get through this week? Every time she looked at Matt, Jodie, or Adam, she would be reminded of what happened the night before. . . .

It had started when Sarah took the bus to the mall, to get a pair of thermal underwear at the sporting-goods store. She'd found what she needed and was walking down an aisle toward the cashier when a fishing rod suddenly came down in front of her.

"Looks like you have to pay a toll," Adam had said, stepping out from behind a display of rods and reels.

Sarah had gazed up into his handsome dark-blue eyes. "How much?"

"Four million dollars," Adam had said.

Sarah had pretended to search her pockets. "Oh, gee, I'm a few dollars short."

"Then how about a slice of pizza?"

"Deal," she had said.

It turned out that Adam had also gone to the sporting-goods store to buy some things for the trip. They went to the pizza place, and each had a slice and a Coke. Adam talked excitedly about their upcoming trip. Sarah just listened and watched. Adam was definitely better-looking, and a little more easygoing, than Matt, and sometimes, deep in Sarah's heart, she wished she'd met him first. But Adam was going with Jodie, and she was going with Matt, and she just had to accept that, didn't she?

After Adam finished talking about the trip, they talked for a while about the track meet that afternoon. It was a home meet, and Adam and Jodie had come to cheer Sarah on.

"Does Matt know you finished first in the mile?" Adam asked.

Sarah shook her head and glanced down at the table. Matt hadn't come to the meet. She'd asked him to, but he'd said he was too busy getting ready for the trip.

Adam must have sensed that he'd touched on a sensitive subject, because he began to ask her about Middletown and her life before she'd moved. He seemed much more interested in her past than Matt ever was. They must've talked for more than an hour, telling each other things they'd never been able to before, because Jodie or Matt was always around. And the more Sarah and Adam talked, the more she liked him and wished that somehow he could be her boyfriend and not Jodie's.

Then the lights in the pizza place went out, and they realized the mall was closing. Adam offered her a ride home.

They parked outside Sarah's house in the dark and kept talking. Adam was funny and smart, and

Sarah couldn't help feeling drawn to him. She strongly suspected that he felt that way toward her, too.

"Well," he finally said, looking into her eyes. "I'm glad we ran into each other."

"I know," Sarah said. "This has been really nice."

"I wish we could talk like this more often," Adam said.

Sarah did too, but she didn't say it. She was filled with regret as she reached down to undo her seat belt. She hated to leave him, but had no choice. She pushed on the seat belt's release and frowned. No matter how hard she pushed on the release, it wouldn't open. Adam saw her struggling.

"It always gets stuck," he said, leaning toward her and squeezing the release with all his might. The seat belt popped open, and Adam glanced up at her. Their faces were only inches apart.

The next thing Sarah knew, she took his face in her hands and gave him a long, slow, lingering kiss.

Sarah dreamed she was sitting in a clearing in the woods. The sky above was bright blue and dotted with small, puffy white, cotton-ball clouds. There were other people around, wearing bell-bottom jeans, and brightly colored tie-dyed T-shirts, and buckskin jackets with long fringes. Their hair was long and parted in the middle, and they wore headbands. A pretty girl with large brown eyes and dirty blond hair was playing with several long strands of tiny, colorful plastic beads that hung from her neck. A boy with shoulder-length black hair was playing a beautiful red wooden guitar, and someone else was throwing a Frisbee to a small black-and-white dog, which was wearing a red bandanna around its neck. Sarah was looking down at her hand, at a ring she was wearing on one of her fingers. Somehow she knew it was a mood ring, and that the stone in it changed colors depending on her mood.

As Sarah stared at the stone, she watched it turn black. . . .

Sarah woke with a start and sat up in bed. Her heart was pounding. The room was pitch black, but she sensed immediately that something was wrong.

"Jodie?" she whispered.

There was no answer.

*"Jodie!"* she hissed more loudly.

Still no answer. The only sound in the room was the thumping of Sarah's heart. Was something wrong? Why hadn't Jodie answered her? Slowly, she slipped out of her bed and crept toward Jodie's bed, then felt the covers in the dark.

Jodie wasn't there!

Where was she? Why had she left Sarah without telling her? It must have been four o'clock in the morning. Where could Jodie have gone at that hour? Sarah reached over and turned on the reading light next to the bed. The door to the bathroom was closed, but she could see light coming from under it. Sarah hurried over and knocked.

"Jodie?"

Again there was no answer.

Sarah pushed open the bathroom door. The bathroom was empty. She was just about to close the door when she noticed something lying on the counter. A ring . . . Sarah stepped into the bathroom and picked it up. Suddenly she felt a shiver. It was just like the ring she'd dreamed about. How was it possible?

She heard a slight rattling sound. Sarah rushed out of the bathroom. Across the room, the doorknob was slowly turning.

# Chapter 9

Sarah tried to scream, but the sound got caught in her throat. The doorknob continued to turn, and the door began to creak open. Sarah's heart was beating so hard she thought she'd die.

Someone stuck her head into the room. . . .

It was Jodie, wearing only the long man's T-shirt she used as a nightgown.

A wave of relief washed over Sarah.

"You're up," Jodie said as she strolled into the room. She was munching on some potato chips from a bag in her hand. "Sorry, I tried not to wake you."

Suddenly, feeling weak in the knees, Sarah plopped down hard on the corner of Jodie's bed. She wondered why she'd felt so overcome with panic a few moments ago. It was so unlike her. In tense situations she was usually quite calm.

"Where did you go?" she asked.

"You know, with being lost and everything, we completely forgot about dinner," Jodie said. "I woke up starved a little while ago. Then I remembered the candy machine in the hall." She held the bag out to Sarah. "Want some chips?"

Sarah shook her head in wonder. "You went out in the hall dressed like that?"

Jodie grinned. "I remembered that guy said the place wasn't open yet. I doubted I'd run into anyone at this time of night." She emptied the last of the chips into her mouth, then crumpled up the bag. "That should hold me till morning."

Sarah was still trying to calm down from the scare she'd just had. She realized the ring was still clenched tightly in her fist. She opened her hand and held the ring out to Jodie.

"Is this yours?" Sarah asked.

Jodie shook her head.

"Are you sure?" Sarah asked.

"Yeah." Jodie looked surprised. "I think I'd know if it was mine. I swear I never saw it before."

Sarah stared down at the ring in her hand. "I . . . I just found it on the counter in the bathroom."

"Well, I didn't leave it there," Jodie said, and she started to get under the covers.

What was the ring doing in their bathroom? How was it possible that she'd dreamed about it only minutes before? And what about that dream?

It had seemed so vivid and real, and yet she knew she'd never seen anything like that before. Sarah felt a tremor of fear. Ever since last night, it seemed that she knew about names and places and things she'd never known before. It almost felt as if she was living someone else's life.

Sarah got back into bed. She was still holding the ring. Not knowing what else to do with it, she slipped it onto her ring finger. It was a perfect fit.

Sarah woke up at about nine thirty. Despite several hours of sleep, she felt almost as tired as when her head had first hit the pillow the night before. Across the room, Jodie was sitting in a chair by the window, with a thick book in her lap.

"Been up long?" Sarah asked with a yawn.

"Not very," Jodie replied.

"What's it like outside?"

"Still raining."

"Are the guys up?"

"I haven't checked."

Sarah lay in bed a few moments more. The sheets felt warm and cozy, but soon the dread of another day with Adam, Jodie, and Matt at this strange inn replaced the comfortable feeling. She got out of bed and walked to the bathroom.

Sarah placed her hand on the doorknob, but it wouldn't turn.

"Did you lock this or something?" Sarah asked.

"Huh?" Jodie looked up from her book.

"The bathroom door's locked," Sarah said.

"Well, I didn't lock it," Jodie said.

Sarah tried the door yet again. The knob wouldn't budge.

"Maybe it's just stuck," Jodie said.

Sarah tried to pull on the door, but it stayed firmly closed. "What should I do?" she asked.

"Let me see," Jodie said, getting up and joining Sarah at the door. As Sarah watched, Jodie reached for the doorknob and turned it. The bathroom door swung open.

"Try turning the doorknob next time," Jodie said, and went back to her chair.

Sarah stared in amazement at the open door. She knew it had been locked, and yet Jodie had opened it with no problem. Something very weird was going on.

A few minutes later Sarah stood in the shower. The hot water felt soothing, and Sarah started to relax again. Maybe she'd just turned the doorknob in the wrong direction. At any rate, it was nothing to get worried about. She used the tiny bottle of shampoo the inn had supplied to wash her red hair.

When she came out of the bathroom, she almost felt refreshed and normal. While she was in the bathroom, Jodie had dressed in jeans and a sweater.

"I bet you wish you had a hair dryer now," Jodie said.

"You're right," Sarah said. Her thick red hair

was a tangle of wet, scraggly curls.

"Well, I'll go check on the guys while you get dressed," Jodie said. "See you in a bit." Sarah watched as Jodie let herself out of the room. Recalling what had just happened with the bathroom door, Sarah locked the door behind Jodie, then tested it to make sure it was closed. The knob wouldn't budge, and when she pulled on the door, it remained firmly shut.

Sarah took her time dressing, then spent a while trying to work a comb through her tangled hair. She was in no rush to join the others. She had just finished combing out her hair when she heard a sound at the door. She stood across the room and watched in amazement as the doorknob started to turn. How was that possible? She'd just locked it a few minutes ago. None of them had been given any keys. . . .

Now the door started to open. Sarah held her breath.

"Jodie?"

The door stopped, partway open, but there was no answer. Sarah stared at the door and swallowed. Had it just opened on its own? Was someone else there? That strange gray-haired guy? He would have been the only one with a key.

Something began to come in through the doorway. At first it looked like the tips of a couple of pointy sticks. Then Sarah realized they were deer horns, and started to relax.

"Very funny, Matt," she said. He must have gotten the key to the room somehow.

The door opened more. Now a black nose and a gray snout came through.

"Hello, dear," a deep voice said. A second later Matt stepped in, grinning and carrying a deer head.

"Get it?" he said. "Hello, deer?"

Sarah rolled her eyes. "You're just a riot, Matt."

Matt's expression grew grim. "You used to like my jokes, Sarah."

Sarah sighed. "I'm sorry. Maybe this just isn't the right time or place."

"Or maybe I'm just not the right person," Matt said.

Sarah felt her body go tense. What had he meant by that? She was about to ask him when Jodie came back in, followed by Adam. Both of them looked perplexed. Sarah felt a tremor. Had Adam told Jodie about him and Sarah?

"The long-haired guy's gone," Adam said, sitting down on the edge of the bed.

"What do you mean?" Sarah asked.

"I mean, I got up an hour ago and searched the whole place and I couldn't find him," Adam said.

"Or anyone else," Jodie added.

"Do you think he called to get the car towed?" Sarah asked.

Matt shrugged. "Who knows?"

"Why don't we call?" Sarah asked.

"See a phone?" Adam replied.

Sarah looked around and realized there was no phone in the room.

"I bet this is one of those places where people go to really get away from it all," Matt said. "Like Club Med."

"But even Club Meds have phones," said Jodie.

"There's a phone," Adam said. "But it's in the office in the lobby, and the door's locked."

Sarah almost asked what they should do next, but it was obvious no one had a clue. It seemed like they were stuck in the inn.

"I guess we'll just have to hang around until either the gray-haired guy gets back or a tow truck shows up with Matt's car," Adam finally said.

Now Matt flopped back on the bed and folded his hands behind his head. "I'll tell you one thing. If I have to be stuck somewhere, this is definitely the place. There's a whole spa out in back, with a swimming pool, hot tub, workout room, squash court, everything. I could really get used to this."

"I don't think we should push our luck," Adam said. "After all, the guy was nice enough to let us stay for free last night."

"Okay," Matt said. But then he grinned. "On the other hand, if we get bored, at least there's stuff to do."

Adam stood up. "I'm going back down to the

office, just to see if maybe he's showed up." He turned to the others. "Anyone want to come?"

Sarah realized he was looking straight at her. The urge to go with him was suddenly strong. She started to say she would go, but then caught herself, remembering the crack Matt had made a few minutes before about him being the wrong person. She didn't want to do anything to arouse his suspicions.

"I'll go with you," Jodie said.

"I saw a big-screen television in that room down at the end of the hall," Matt said. "It's next to the game room, with all the videos. Why don't we meet down there?"

It sounded like a good idea. Adam and Jodie headed off to the office. Sarah wished it had been her instead of Jodie. Without a word to Sarah, Matt stood up and headed toward the door.

"Uh, Matt?" Sarah said.

"Yeah?" Matt stopped in the doorway.

"Could I have the key?"

He frowned. "What key?"

"The one you used to open the door."

"What are you talking about?" Matt asked. "I didn't use a key. The door was open."

Sarah stared at him. "Matt, I locked the door myself."

"Well, maybe you did," Matt replied with an angry shrug. "But it was open when I got there."

It wasn't possible, she thought. Not only had

she locked it, but she'd tested it herself.

"Matt, you're not kidding me, are you?" she asked. "I mean, this isn't another one of your jokes, is it?"

"No way, Sarah," Matt said. "I'm not wasting any more of my jokes on you."

Sarah shook her head, dismayed. "Matt, why do you have to be like this?"

"Look who's talking," Matt said, and left.

# Chapter 10

They spent the rest of the morning watching television, and eating the Fig Newtons and Mallomars Jodie had packed. Matt had wanted to play the video games, but the machines weren't hooked up yet. Adam and Jodie had come back from the office after finding the gray-haired guy still hadn't returned. Jodie sat on a couch in the back of the room and read *David Copperfield*. Sarah felt bored and uncomfortable around Matt, who was obviously mad at her. She was also tense about being in this inn, with no one else around and all these weird things happening. But as long as the others were watching television and reading, she was willing to let the time pass.

Finally, in the middle of a soap opera, Adam stood up.

"This is crazy," he said.

"What is?" Matt asked.

"Us sitting here watching television and waiting for this guy to come back," Adam said. "At least let's go see if anyone's towed your car out of the ditch."

"If they did, they'd bring it here," Jodie said.

"How do you know?" Adam asked.

"Hey, sit down," Matt said. "What's the point of getting uptight? We've got entertainment, junk food . . . this is heaven."

"Maybe for you," Adam said. "But we're supposed to be going on a fishing trip to my uncle's cabin, not hanging around in some inn."

"Considering the fact that it's still raining outside, I'd be just as happy to stay here," Matt said.

"Well, I'm gonna go check on the car," Adam said. "Anyone want to come?"

Once again he stared right at Sarah, and she felt that same yearning just to be alone with him. Maybe this time she could. Matt was so busy watching television he probably wouldn't care. And Jodie was still buried in her book. Sarah was just about to say she'd go when Jodie closed her book.

"My eyes are starting to hurt," she said, getting up. "I guess I could use a break."

For a long moment Adam's and Sarah's eyes met. *He wanted me to go with him*, she thought. But it was too late. Adam and Jodie headed out of the room.

Sarah suddenly felt a wave of anger wash over her. Why did Jodie always get to go with Adam? Why didn't *she* ever get to go?

"Don't get lost," Matt called after them.

*   *   *

Two more hours passed. Sarah watched more soap operas and absentmindedly twisted the mood ring around her finger, as she stewed over the fact that Jodie had gone off with Adam. Suddenly she looked down at the ring. The stone was green—the color of jealousy. Sarah realized the stone was right. She was jealous of Jodie. And yet she had no right to be. Jodie was Adam's girlfriend, not Sarah. Sarah didn't want that creepy ring on her hand. She tried to slide it off, but it wouldn't go past the knuckle. Sarah didn't get it. The night before it had slid on easily, almost as if it were made for her. Now, no matter how hard she tried, she couldn't get the ring off her finger.

Sarah thought of asking Matt for help, but decided against it. It would be too difficult to explain where the ring had come from in the first place. The way Matt was sitting and staring at the television reminded Sarah of her father. She waited for him to say something, but all he did was stare at the screen and ignore her. Given the situation, Sarah might not have minded, but she felt other concerns growing inside her.

"I'm worried about Jodie and Adam," she finally said. "They should've been back by now."

"Don't worry, they'll be back," Matt said tersely.

"It's going to be dark soon," Sarah said.

"Not that soon," Matt said. "I'm sure they'll be back way before then."

When another half hour passed, and Jodie and Adam still hadn't returned, Sarah looked out the window and saw that the rain had slackened and only a light mist was drifting through the bare trees. She shifted in her chair and felt as if she was going crazy sitting in that room.

"I'm still worried about them, Matt," she said. "Maybe they're lost. I really think we should take a look."

"Go ahead," Matt said with a shrug.

"Won't you come?" Sarah asked.

"What's the point?" Matt asked. "You know they have to come back. It's not like there's anyplace else they can go."

Sarah supposed he was right, but she didn't understand why he was being so cold and aloof. She wanted to ask, but she was afraid of what he might say. In the meantime, Jodie and Adam had been gone so long. Sarah knew she wasn't really worried about them. The truth was, she suddenly couldn't stand the idea of them being alone for so long.

"I'm going out to look for them," she said.

"Have a good time," Matt said, without looking up from the television.

Adam stared at the side of the muddy road and took a deep breath of damp air. "It has to be here."

"Adam, we've been up and down this road twice already," Jodie said. "We've gone all the way back to where the pavement ended. It's just not here."

"It doesn't make sense," Adam said. "If someone came with a tow truck, they were supposed to bring the car to the inn."

"Well, maybe they got the message mixed up," Jodie said. "Or maybe there was something wrong with Matt's car. Maybe they had to take it into the shop to fix it."

Adam shook his head in disgust. "The shop? Wonderful. We'll never get to my uncle's cabin now."

Jodie shivered as a thick wave of mist floated across the road. What she really wanted to do was go back to that nice warm inn. If they'd made it to Adam's uncle's cabin they'd probably be huddling around an old iron stove, just trying to stay warm. She was starting to think that Matt was right. Maybe being stuck at the New Arcadia was a stroke of good luck.

"Well, come on," she said. "Let's go back. The fog's getting heavier, and the sun's already setting. I really don't want to get lost."

Together, she and Adam started back down the road. Ahead of them waves of fog drifted across the muddy road and disappeared into the woods.

"You know what's strange?" Adam said as they walked. "We've walked up and down this road twice, and we haven't seen a single living creature. Not even a deer, or raccoon, or any birds."

"Maybe they're all staying inside today," Jodie said.

Adam smirked. It was pretty clear what Jodie had on her mind. She didn't care about getting to the cabin, she just wanted to be back in the inn. As they walked along the side of the road, skirting the puddles, Adam happened to glance to his left, into the dark woods. Suddenly he stopped.

"What is it?" Jodie asked.

Adam blinked, then rubbed his eyes. "Nothing."

"Did you see something?"

Adam nodded. "For a second, I thought I did."

"Maybe something lives around here, after all," Jodie said, looking around.

They started walking again. After half a dozen yards Adam abruptly stopped again, this time certain he'd seen something red out of the corner of his eye. But when he turned, it was gone.

"Thought you saw it again?" Jodie asked.

Adam nodded. "It was red. Like a cardinal. Only, I'm pretty sure it wasn't a cardinal."

They kept walking. Suddenly, between the damp brown tree trunks, Adam saw another flash of red. Only it wasn't red feathers. It was red curly hair . . . hair the same color as Sarah's.

"Look!" he whispered, grabbing Jodie's arm and stopping her. He pressed his finger to his lips and then pointed at the place between the trees where he'd seen it.

A moment later he caught another glimpse of it.

"There!" he hissed, pointing toward another spot in the trees.

Jodie squinted and tried to follow his line of sight. "I didn't see it."

"There!"

"Where, Adam?"

It disappeared again. Then quickly reappeared. Adam couldn't figure out what was going on.

"There!"

"I still don't see it."

"It's moving parallel to us," Adam said. "Deep in the woods. I'm just catching a glimpse of it every now and—"

"I saw it!" Jodie gasped. "A flash of red hair."

There was only one person they knew who had hair like that.

"Sarah!" Adam shouted.

"You think she decided to take a run through the woods?" Jodie asked. "She said she used to do that a lot."

"I guess." Adam shrugged and cupped his hands around his mouth. "Hey, Sarah!"

Again they saw her flash through the trees.

"*Sarah!*" Adam shouted more loudly.

"She has to hear you," Jodie said. "Why doesn't she answer?"

"I don't know," Adam said, stepping down off the road. "But I'm going to find out."

# Chapter 11

Sarah knew that her sudden jealousy of Jodie made no sense, and yet she couldn't control it. Maybe it was because she knew Adam wanted to be with her, not Jodie. She had seen it in his eyes. Something else was driving her a bit crazy as well —the odd sensation that she'd been here before, that she somehow knew this place. And yet she was certain she'd never been there. Her parents hardly ever took her on trips, but when they did, it was almost always to a big city where a business convention was taking place.

Outside, the damp, misty air sent a chill through her jacket and sweatshirt as she walked up the cobblestone driveway. When she reached the sign welcoming her to the New Arcadia, she turned and looked back at the inn. It was half hidden in the gradually thickening mist, but yes, she was almost certain she'd seen it before.

But how? And where?

Maybe in a magazine.

But that didn't explain how she'd known the name *Arcadia* last night, before Adam had found the sign, or why the double-headed arrow nailed to the tree had seemed so familiar.

For several minutes Sarah stood by the sign. She had intended to walk back up the unpaved road and look for Jodie and Adam, but now a strange new thought suddenly burst into her mind: *Take a run in the woods*.

Sarah recoiled at the idea. Run in the woods, now? No, she had told herself she wanted to go find Adam and Jodie and see what they were up to. But she could feel an urge sweeping through her, just as strong as the urge the night she'd kissed Adam.

Well, maybe she could take a short run in the woods. Just around the inn a few times. By the time she got back, if Jodie and Adam still hadn't returned, she'd go up the road and look for them.

Sarah stepped off the driveway and started to jog through the thick brush between the trees. After a few steps she slowed down. The brush ahead was too thick. Maybe taking a run wasn't such a good idea after all. Suddenly she found herself picking up speed again, running to the left. But why? The next thing she knew, she'd found a thin trail on the other side of a thick stand of birches. The trail made a clear path through the brush and trees. But how had she known it was there? She couldn't have seen it through the birches, and yet somehow, she'd run straight toward it as if she'd known it was there all her life.

Sarah started down the trail, feeling frightened, but also determined to try to understand what in the world was happening to her. There had been too many coincidences. Too many things she'd couldn't have known about, but somehow did.

Sarah felt as though some mysterious force was pushing her. And that same force assured her there was nothing to be afraid of.

The trail started to run alongside a thin stream, hardly more than a foot or two wide. It bubbled and gurgled over dark greenish rocks. Soon the stream widened and formed a pool in a place where someone had dammed it up with stones. The pool was about thirty feet wide, with sand and pebbles on the bottom. Sarah slowed down and looked for the diving rock, a tall gray rock you could stand on to jump into the pool.

*Wait a minute!*

How did she know about the diving rock?

She didn't have a clue, and yet there it was, plain as day on the other side of the pool.

Sarah stared at the rock and then down through the clear water at the sandy bottom of the pool. As she listened to the sound of the water running down over the rocks, she imagined hearing the distant sounds of laughter and shouting, and someone strumming a guitar. Reflected on the surface of the pool, she could see a blue sky dotted with white clouds. Then there was a bare-chested boy, with beads around his neck and long blond hair falling down over his forehead in thick bangs.

*Doug . . .*

A sudden rush of emotions swept through her. Love, jealousy, need . . .

*Doug . . . I love you.*

Sarah blinked. The reflection disappeared. She looked up, and saw that the sky above was gray. This was too weird for words. She shook her head. Doug was gone. But who was he, and why had she felt those strong feelings for him? Wait, weren't they just like the feelings she had for Adam? Maybe that was it. Sarah suddenly yawned. Maybe it was just fatigue. She'd hardly gotten any sleep the past two nights, and it was obviously starting to have an effect on her imagination.

No longer feeling the urge to run, Sarah decided to head back to the inn. Not far back up the trail, the path split in two directions. One seemed to go toward the road, the other appeared to head more toward the inn. Sarah took the latter, walking quickly now, because she wanted to see if Adam and Jodie were back.

Suddenly the trail ended in a clearing about

forty feet in diameter, which was covered with beaten-down brownish grass. Sarah stopped and looked around in shock. Could it be? Could this be the place she'd dreamed about? Where they played guitar and threw Frisbees to dogs?

How could she have known about all this—The Arcadia, and the diving rock, and this clearing? It seemed impossible. Unless she'd had another life she knew nothing about . . .

Then something colorful in the brown grass caught her eye. Sarah bent down and her fingers closed around a string of tiny, brightly colored plastic beads.

*Just like the beads the pretty girl with the dirty blond hair in her dream had worn. But this was no dream. Like the mood ring, the beads in her hand were real.*

This was getting too weird. Sarah turned and started to run back up the trail through the woods. It was all too familiar and too strange. She'd never been to the New Arcadia before. She couldn't have been there before. And yet . . . and yet . . .

Suddenly she felt a pair of arms go around her roughly as someone stepped out from behind a tree and grabbed her from behind.

# Chapter 12

"Help!" Sarah screamed, trying to fight loose.

"Sarah, it's me. Cut it out!" The voice sounded familiar. Sarah stopped struggling and turned around. It was Adam!

There she was, in his arms, her heart beating wildly, looking up into his deep-blue eyes. They were both breathing hard. *Love . . . jealousy . . . need.* Sarah was aware of feeling emotions far more intense than anything she'd ever felt for Matt or any other boy. She just wanted to hold him tight and never ever let go. Sarah felt her arms start to rise. She knew she was going to slide them around his neck. She wanted to feel his lips against hers. *She had to feel them!*

"Did you catch her?" It was Jodie, calling from somewhere close by in the woods.

Adam let go of Sarah, and they backed away from each other, both still gasping for breath. A second later, Jodie came through the trees toward them.

"Yeah, I caught her," Adam said, then turned to Sarah again. "What's going on?"

"I . . . I don't know," Sarah answered.

"I must have called you fifty times," Adam said, still panting. "Why didn't you answer?"

"Are you okay?" Jodie asked her, with a concerned look on her face.

"I think so," Sarah said, suddenly feeling horribly guilty. She couldn't meet Jodie's gaze, and she turned to Adam. "I never heard you calling me."

"We've probably been chasing you for ten minutes, yelling our brains out. You just kept running."

"Ten minutes?" Sarah didn't know what he was talking about. "I just started running a few moments ago. I hardly went anywhere."

Jodie and Adam shared a glance. Even as the words left Sarah's mouth, she felt her calves start to tighten up. That was strange. She usually had to run for a while before that happened. Why was she feeling it after running for only a few moments?

Jodie looked at her again. "Are you sure you're okay?" She sounded truly worried.

"Yes, I think so," Sarah said. Despite what she felt in her legs, she was *certain* she hadn't run that long. "You must have been following someone else."

Adam reached toward her shoulder and slid his fingers through her hair. Sarah felt a stirring sensation as his fingertips brushed past her ear.

"With hair identical to yours?"

"You had to hear us," Jodie said.

"I swear I didn't," Sarah replied. She noticed Adam staring at her hand.

"What're those?" he asked.

"Just some beads," Sarah said, holding them up. "I found them in a clearing back there."

Jodie took the beads and studied them. "You know what these are? Love beads."

"What are you talking about, Jodie?" Adam asked.

Jodie slipped them over her head and around her neck. "Everyone wore them in the sixties. I know because my mother saved all hers."

Adam smirked. "Well, I'm really glad you've shared that with us." Then he turned back to Sarah again. "I still don't understand why you kept running away and didn't answer us."

"I swear I only ran for a minute," Sarah said. "Maybe less. And I never heard you calling me."

Adam sighed and shook his head. It didn't make sense, but he wasn't going to argue anymore. "So, what were you doing out here, anyway?"

"I came out to find you two," Sarah said. "It seemed like you were gone much too long."

"That's because we couldn't find the car," Adam said. "We looked everywhere for it. Someone must have come and towed it away."

"The only thing that makes sense is that there was something wrong with it, and they had to take it to the garage and get it fixed," Jodie said.

Sarah nodded. But as far as she was concerned, nothing made sense anymore. Except that, more than ever, she wanted to be with Adam and feel his lips on hers again.

"Well, let's get back to the inn," Adam said. "Maybe that gray-haired guy's come back, and he can tell us what this is all about."

It was pretty dark out when they finally got back to the inn. They found Matt in the television room, still slumped on the couch staring at the tube. When he saw them, he sat up.

"You find the car?" he asked.

"Someone did," Adam replied.

"What do you mean?"

Adam told him they'd searched for the car, and it was gone. Matt started to looked worried.

"Man, I hope no one stole it," he said. "My parents'll kill me."

"Has the gray-haired guy come back?" Adam asked.

Matt shook his head. "Haven't seen him."

"Have you looked?" Jodie asked.

"Well, not exactly," Matt admitted.

"So he could be here in another part of the inn, or in the spa," Jodie said.

"I guess," Matt said.

"I think it's time we find him to find out what happened to the car," Jodie said. "Why don't we break up into teams? Adam and I will look in the spa. You guys look around the inn."

Matt got up. "All right. I'm pretty tired of watching television anyway."

Jodie and Adam left to check the spa, and Matt and Sarah started to walk around the inn. Once again a sense of angry jealousy began to simmer in Sarah, but she tried to force it back down. She had to accept the fact that she was with Matt, and Adam was with Jodie. Besides, she was dying to tell someone about her dream, and the diving rock, and the love beads, and all these other strange things that felt so familiar. Ever since they'd started on this trip, Matt had been strangely distant and curt with her, but he was still the person she was closest to. As they walked down the hall back to the lobby, she decided to take a chance.

"Matt," she began.

"Yeah?"

"Are you okay?"

"I'd be better if I knew where my car was," he said.

"I know, that must be really upsetting," Sarah said.

"Except Jodie's probably right," Matt said. "It probably just got towed to some garage. We went into that ditch pretty hard last night. It wouldn't surprise me if something in the front end got knocked out of whack."

"Are you still mad at me about that?" Sarah asked.

"About the car?" Matt stopped and looked at her. "Well, I don't know. I mean, I wish you hadn't yanked on the steering wheel, but I also know you'd never do anything like that on purpose."

He didn't seem to be as angry at her now.

"I still can't believe none of you saw that bus," Sarah said.

Matt smirked. "And I can't believe you saw it. Come on, let's go look for that guy."

He started to walk again, but Sarah reached out and grabbed his arm to stop him.

Matt frowned. "What is it, Sarah?"

"Matt, I have to tell you something," she said. "It wasn't only the bus. It's been a dozen things. Remember last night when we came to that fork in the road, and I said 'Arcadia' before Adam found that old sign?"

"So?"

"Well, I'd never heard the word before," Sarah said.

"Maybe you caught a glimpse of it before Adam picked it up," Matt said.

"I don't think so," Sarah said. "And last night I dreamed about a clearing in the woods, and hippies sitting around with mood rings and love beads. Well, look." She showed him the mood ring on her finger.

"Where'd you get that?" Matt asked.

"I found it in the bathroom," Sarah said.

"Well, then that explains it," Matt said with a shrug.

"But it doesn't explain why I dreamed about it, and how it got into the bathroom," Sarah said. "I dreamed about a clearing and someone wearing love beads, and just now when I was outside, I walked into the same exact clearing and found some love beads."

"I guess it's just a coincidence," Matt said.

"Matt, it's not. It can't be," Sarah said. "Believe me. Everywhere I look I see things that seem familiar. But I'm certain I've never been here before."

Matt scratched his head. "Well, then what do you think's going on?"

"I don't know, Matt, but I'm starting to freak out." As Sarah said this, she couldn't help yawning.

"Does this inn look familiar?" Matt asked.

Sarah nodded. "From the outside."

"What about inside?"

Sarah thought for a moment. Even the inside felt familiar, although she didn't remember the colors of the walls or things like that. "A little."

"Okay, look," Matt said, taking her hand. "Close your eyes. Now I'm going to lead you somewhere and you try to imagine what it looks like."

"Okay." Sarah kept her eyes closed while Matt led her down the hall by the hand.

He stopped. "You're in the lobby, Sarah. Now

what's the most distinctive thing that comes to mind about it?"

"Uh, there's a big stone hearth in the corner," Sarah said.

"Doesn't count," Matt said. "You probably saw that last night. What else?"

Sarah tried to concentrate. Suddenly an image of a broad swirling stained-glass ceiling came into her head. It was so vivid and real, she knew it had to be there.

"The ceiling," she said. "It's all stained glass."

"Open your eyes," Matt said.

Sarah opened her eyes and looked up. The ceiling was made up of square, white cork tiles.

"See?" Matt said. "I guess if you imagine enough stuff, some of it's bound to come true. But this place really isn't so familiar, after all."

Sarah was confused, but also somewhat relieved, because it seemed that he could be right. She nodded and yawned again.

"You look pretty tired," Matt said. "Maybe you should go back to your room and take a nap."

Sarah hesitated. She was nervous about being alone in the inn. Well, maybe she wouldn't mind as much if she were in her room with the door locked.

"You're right," she said. "But I'd really feel better if you'd give me the key. I mean, it's not that I don't trust you, Matt, but—"

"What key, Sarah?" Matt asked.

"The key to my room," Sarah said. "I know

you have to have it, because you unlocked the door before."

"I told you the door was open," Matt said. "I swear there's no key."

Sarah stared him. Was he lying? She was positive she had locked the door. She could remember how the knob wouldn't turn.

"Matt, I'm serious, please give me the key."

Suddenly his expression changed. She could see she'd made him angry again. "You don't believe me, do you? Boy, Sarah, I really appreciate how much you trust me."

The words reeked of sarcasm. Sarah's mouth fell open, but no words came out. Matt turned and walked away.

# Chapter 13

It was summer. The grass was green, the branches of the trees were heavy with leaves, and there wasn't a cloud in the clear blue sky. Sarah was walking through the woods. She was barefoot and she could feel the soft, cool dirt of the trail and the occasional hard sensation of a rock or twig. The trail started to follow a small brook, and she watched the water rippling down over the rocks, its surface shimmering with sunlight.

The brook ended at a small dammed-up pool, whose surface was as smooth and unbroken as a mirror. Ahead of her, a stocky boy wearing a leather vest and a pair of cut-off blue jeans sat on the diving rock, playing a red guitar. He had long black hair that fell to his broad, muscular shoulders.

*Mike . . .*

He was singing and strumming with his eyes closed. He didn't hear her walking up quietly behind him. She felt something round and long in her hand. Looking down, she saw it was the green handle of a long knife with a gray steel blade. As she got closer, she hid the knife behind her back. Mike must've heard her, because he suddenly stopped playing and turned around.

"Hi," he said, smiling. He had large white teeth that almost looked too big compared to his other features.

"Hi, Mike," she heard herself reply.

"Going for a swim, huh?" Mike said.

"Maybe," she said. "Or maybe I'll just listen to you play."

"You sure?" he seemed a little uncertain.

"I'm sure," she said, squeezing the knife handle behind her back. "Go on, I love the music."

"Well, all right." Mike grinned, then closed his eyes and started to strum the guitar again.

Without warning, she lifted the knife and watched its shadow rise against Mike's dark-brown vest. . . .

"Ahhh!" Sarah woke with a scream. Her heart was beating a mile a minute and her forehead was damp with sweat.

*Calm down*, she told herself. *It was only a dream*.

But she never had dreams that were that vivid, or felt so real. She slipped off the bed. She had only lain down for a nap, and was still wearing her clothes. She bent down and slid on her hiking boots.

It was time to find someone who knew what was going on.

The gray-haired man wasn't anywhere to be found, so Matt decided to go over to the spa and try to hook up with Adam and Jodie. Unlike the inn, which was sort of old and renovated to look new, the spa was completely modern. Built mostly of glass and steel, it must have spanned nearly an acre.

Leaving the inn, Matt pushed through two metal doors and walked down a brightly lit hall. The gray-blue carpet smelled new, and the cream-colored paint on the walls was obviously fresh. As Matt walked along, a new scent entered his nostrils: chlorine. He stopped at a stainless-steel door marked "Pool," and looked inside through a small round window.

This wasn't the first time he'd seen the pool. He'd seen it that morning, when he and Adam had explored the place. Matt had been particularly interested in the hot tub, but Adam was too intent on finding the gray-haired man to inspect it. Now was Matt's chance to take a closer look. If there was one thing he loved, it was kicking back in the hot tub, turning on the whirlpool and soaking in the heat.

The hot tub was enclosed in a separate glass

area, and as Matt went through the glass door, he was immediately disappointed. The air wasn't warm and steamy, which meant the water in the hot tub wasn't hot. Everything else about the tub was perfect, though. It was nice and big, and he could see that it was deep, which was great when you really wanted to get your whole body submerged.

Then Matt noticed the gray metal box on the wall marked "Controls." He opened it. Inside were an on/off switch and two dials. One was marked "Heat," the other "Pressure."

Matt smiled.

Should he?

Hey, why not?

He flicked the switch, and the water in the tub began to swirl and gurgle. Then he adjusted the pressure and turned the heat dial up to one hundred degrees. Great, that would really get this thing cooking.

While Matt waited for the water to heat up, he went through another stainless-steel door marked "Men's Locker Room." Inside, he found a bunch of soft, fluffy white towels and a small tube of shampoo. He knew you weren't supposed to shampoo in the hot tub, but his hair had gotten all matted down from the rain the night before, and he figured one quick shampoo wouldn't gum up the filters too much.

Back in the hot tub room, the air had grown

warm and moist, steaming up the glass walls that separated it from the swimming pool. Matt stripped down to his undershorts and stuck his toe in. With a jerk, he immediately pulled it out. Wow, the water had gotten hot fast. The water system must have been hooked up to one mean heating plant. But hot was just the way he liked it.

Matt sat down at the edge of the tub and very slowly eased one foot into the water. He was just about to start submerging the other foot when he looked up and noticed someone walk past the steamed-up window. From her height and the red hair, he had no doubt that it was Sarah.

For a moment, he wasn't sure if he wanted to call her or not. Then he decided he did. He quickly got up and wrapped a towel around his waist, but by the time he pushed open the glass door and looked out around the pool, she was gone.

"Sarah?" he shouted. "Hey, Sarah!"

No one answered. Matt let the glass door close. That was weird, he thought. If she saw the glass all steamed up, it should have been a dead giveaway that someone was inside. Why hadn't she stopped?

Sarah didn't know what it was about this place that made her imagine and dream all these strange things, but she knew she felt better being with her friends than being alone. She was also hoping that they could help her figure out why the New Arcadia was having this weird effect on her. Jodie and Adam had said they were going to look for the gray-haired guy in the spa, so she decided to try there first.

She stopped in the weight room, the aerobics studio, and the squash court before she came to the pool. She pushed open the door and looked in. The pool was empty, and she was just about to leave when she noticed that the glass at the far end of the pool area was steamed up.

Curious, she went to see what was inside. She pushed through the steam-covered glass door and was startled to find Matt sitting at the edge of a hot tub, wearing only his undershorts.

"Oops!" Matt quickly pulled a white towel onto his lap. "So there you are. How come you stopped in this time, and not before?"

"Before?" Sarah frowned. "What are you talking about?"

"About three minutes ago you walked right past here," Matt said. "I tried to call you, but by the time I got to the door, you were gone."

Sarah stared at him in disbelief. "Matt, I've never been in here before."

"Oh, come on, Sarah, I saw you," Matt said.

Sarah stared back at the glass door. Earlier, Jodie and Adam had insisted that they'd chased after her for nearly ten minutes through the woods. Now Matt was saying that she'd already passed the door once. Sarah wondered if her friends might be playing some kind of joke on her.

"Are you sure it was me?" Sarah asked.

"You know anyone else staying here that has bright-red hair?" Matt asked.

Before Sarah could answer, the glass door swung open. Jodie and Adam came in with grim looks on their faces.

# Chapter 14

"I thought you two were going to look for the gray-haired guy in the inn," Adam said. "Not hang out in the hot tub."

"I did," Matt said. "I couldn't find him anywhere, so I came over here. I was gonna meet up with you guys, but then I found this hot tub."

"Great, Matt. How's that going to help us get back on the road to my uncle's cabin?" Adam asked.

"Well, I just wanted to try it," Matt said sheepishly.

Adam turned to Sarah. "How about you?"

"I haven't seen anyone," Sarah said. "I just got here a second ago."

It was suddenly important to Sarah that Adam not think she was present when Matt stripped down to his underwear. "Did you have any luck?"

Adam and Jodie shook their heads.

"It's really strange," Jodie said. "First the gray-haired guy disappears, then the car."

"Hey, listen, if he wants to trade this place for the car, that's fine with me," Matt said. "I bet my parents wouldn't mind, either."

Adam gave him a stony look.

"Hey, I'm not saying I don't want to go to your uncle's wonderful cabin," Matt said. "I'm just saying as long as we're stuck here, why not enjoy the place?"

"Maybe he's right," Jodie said. "Sooner or later, we're bound to get the car back. In the meantime, why not relax and have a little fun?"

"Well, I don't know about the rest of you, but one thing I'd like to do is eat," Adam said. "I'm starving."

"I hate to say it, but we've run out of Mallomars and Fig Newtons," Jodie added.

"I've still got the freeze-dried scrambled eggs in my pack," Sarah said.

Adam groaned. "I don't mind the idea of them out in the woods, but here at this fancy inn, I'd like to do better."

They waited out in the hall for Matt to get dressed. Out of the corner of her eye Sarah watched Adam and Jodie for signs of how they were getting along. When Jodie touched Adam's arm, Sarah found herself growing jealous again. It was so strange. She'd seen Jodie and Adam touch dozens of times, and never felt the least bit jealous. But ever since Adam had kissed her, everything had changed.

"Sometimes I really don't understand Matt," Adam said in a low voice while they waited. "It's like he never seems to take anything seriously."

"I think he just expects everything to work out," Jodie said. "I mean, in one sense, I think he's right. It's really not so bad being here."

Adam gave her a sour look.

"I think you're just upset because you really had your heart set on getting to your uncle's cabin for the week, and on fishing," Jodie told him.

"Maybe they have fishing here," Sarah said.

Adam gave her an offhanded shrug. "Yeah, you're right. Maybe I am taking this all too seriously."

The glass doors swung open, and Matt came out. "Okay, I'm ready. I promise I won't sleep until we find that guy, get my car back, and spend the rest of the week sitting in your uncle's cabin in the freezing rain."

Even Adam had to smile. He slapped Matt on the back. "Let's just find something to eat."

They were crossing through the lobby when the inn's front door opened and the gray-haired man came in, wearing a green rain suit and carrying a fishing rod and an old-fashioned brown wicker creel.

"How's it going?" he asked, shaking the rain-water off the rain suit and pulling the hood off. It seemed to Sarah that he stared at her again.

"Maybe you ought to tell us," Adam said. "Where's our car?"

"Car?" He looked puzzled for a moment. "Oh, yeah, I called Nathan over at the garage this morning. He said he'd come and tow it over here, unless it needed some work, in which case he'd take it into the shop."

"I guess that means it needed some work." Matt groaned.

The gray-haired guy looked at his watch and nodded. "Too late to call now. I'll have to try him again in the morning."

It took a moment for the implications of the statement to sink in. Then Adam voiced what Sarah was thinking: "So we have to stay here again tonight?"

The gray-haired guy pulled off the rain suit. Underneath, he was wearing the same clothes he'd worn last night when he met them at the door. "Well, you don't have to stay if you don't want to, dude. But, given the circumstances, you're welcome to." He walked toward Adam and held out his hand. "By the way, my name's Sebastian. I'm the caretaker here."

Adam shook his hand. "It's nice to meet you, Sebastian. I'm Adam."

The others introduced themselves. When it

was Sarah's turn, Sebastian seemed to hold her hand longer than the others. And hers was the only name he repeated. "Sarah, huh? That's a nice name."

Sarah blushed and withdrew her hand from his. Sebastian turned to the others. "You folks eaten yet?"

They shook their heads. Sebastian picked up the creel and opened it. Inside lay half a dozen fresh, speckled trout.

"Hey, those are real beauties," Adam said.

"I think I've got enough for everyone," Sebastian said. "Why don't you give me about half an hour, and then meet me over in the dining room."

Sarah and Jodie gave each other questioning looks, but the idea of freshly cooked trout sounded an awful lot better than freeze-dried scrambled eggs.

"Okay, it sounds good," Sarah said.

"Fine, see you in a bit." Sebastian picked up his rod and rain gear and went through a door marked "Dining Room" at the other end of the lobby.

"I can't believe we have to spend another night in this place," Adam said after Sebastian left.

"You still want to go?" Jodie asked him.

"I can't decide," Adam said. "Half of me says we should get the car and leave. The other half says take it easy and go with the flow." Adam paused for a second. "One question: How come we're having dinner with that guy?"

"I guess we don't have to, if you don't want to," Jodie said. "But it might seem kind of rude, considering that he's letting us stay here."

Adam looked at Matt. "What do you think?"

Matt shrugged. "Don't ask me. Ask Sarah. She's the one he likes."

The next thing Sarah knew, they were all staring at her.

# Chapter 15

"That's not true," Sarah gasped.

"Oh, come on," Matt said. "He wasn't even gonna let us in last night until he saw you. And just now, did you see the way he looked at you? 'Sarah, huh?'" Matt imitated Sebastian's voice. "'That's a nice name.'"

"Wait," Adam said. "Even if it's true, it's not her fault if he likes her."

Sarah appreciated the way Adam defended her, but she was also hurt that Matt had sounded so vindictive. Even though she yearned to be with Adam, she didn't want Matt to be angry with her. Especially not while they were all trapped together on this trip.

"I think we'd better do it," Jodie said. "We only have to be with him for dinner. Besides, I bet that fish will be delicious."

The others nodded.

"I feel like cleaning up a little," Jodie said, turning toward the hall that went to their rooms.

"Me, too," said Adam, following her.

"Me, three," Matt said, starting after him.

But as he turned to leave, Sarah blocked his way. "Maybe we'd better talk."

Matt stopped and scowled at her. "About what?"

"You know," Sarah said.

Matt glanced at Jodie and Adam.

"Oh, okay," Adam said with a smile. "We'll catch you two later."

Matt and Sarah waited until Jodie and Adam left the lobby. She hated the idea of letting Adam think she wanted to be alone with Matt, but she had to clear things with him.

"Okay," Matt said. "What do you want to talk about?"

"Let's sit," Sarah said.

They sat down on a couch in front of the large stone hearth. Matt crossed his arms and stared at the ceiling. He reminded Sarah of the kids she sometimes saw in the office at school, waiting to get bawled out by the principal.

"Ever since we left on this trip yesterday, I've felt like you've been mad at me," Sarah said.

"Oh? What makes you say that?" Matt asked sarcastically.

"Just everything. Especially the way you're acting now."

Matt let out a big breath and stared at the floor.

Then he looked up at Sarah. "Where were you the other night?"

"I—I told you," Sarah said, trying to stay calm. "I went to buy long underwear."

"That's all?" Matt leaned toward her.

"No. I ran into Adam, and we had a slice of pizza."

He eyed her suspiciously. "Why didn't you tell me that before?"

Sarah shrugged. "I don't know. I guess I was afraid you'd be angry."

"Why would I be angry?" Matt asked. "I thought you two were just friends."

"We are," Sarah said. But as she said it, she stared down at the brown carpet.

"So what happened between you and Adam?" Matt asked.

"We talked," Sarah said.

"And?"

"He drove me home."

"*And?*"

"That's all, Matt."

Matt looked her straight in the eye. "You swear?"

Sarah nodded.

Matt leaned back into the couch and slid his hands into his pockets.

"Is that why you've been so mad?" Sarah asked.

"It's part of the reason," Matt said.

"What's the rest?"

As usual, Matt seemed reluctant to talk. He

never wanted to talk about serious things. Sarah knew he was much more comfortable playing games and jokes.

"Talk to me, Matt," Sarah said. She had to find out everything.

"What's the point?"

It was a good question. Ever since the night she'd been with Adam, Sarah had lost any sense of attraction toward Matt. She knew now that she was going to have to break up with him, but she wanted to wait until after the trip was over. It was important to her that they all remained friends. That meant not having any big scenes with Matt, not while Jodie and Adam were around.

"Because I care for you," she told him. "I don't like it when things are tense between us."

Matt let out a deep sigh. "Okay. Here's the story. Last summer when we first started going together, I really thought everything was great. It was just you and me, and we had a good time together. Then Jodie and Adam came back from camp, and it all began to change. At first I thought you were just being shy because you didn't know them. Or maybe you were jealous because Jodie and I used to go together. But then I'd see the way you looked at Adam, and it felt like you wished you were with him and not me."

Sarah reached over and patted his hand with hers. "That's not true, Matt. I've always liked you more than him."

*Liar*, she thought. Even as the words left her lips, she wished it were Adam and not Matt she was sitting with.

Matt looked up at her. "You mean it?"

"Yes."

"One hundred percent?"

Sarah nodded.

Matt grinned. "Well, that's more like it."

He started to slide closer to her on the couch. Suddenly Sarah realized he wanted to put his arm around her and kiss her. Before he could, she quickly got up and walked toward the stone hearth. There was a large pile of logs beside it.

"It's kind of chilly in here," she said, rubbing her arms as if she were cold. "Wouldn't it be nice to build a fire?"

"Now?" Matt asked, surprised.

"Sure. Why not?"

"Well, I guess we could." Matt stood up and walked toward the woodpile. Sarah watched as he picked up a log and placed it in the hearth. He turned to the pile to get another log, but stopped.

"Hey, cool," he said, lifting up something long and narrow. Sarah realized it was a sheath for a knife. It had been lying under the log Matt had moved, hidden from sight. She watched as Matt grabbed the green knife handle and pulled the knife out of the sheath. The blade was gray steel.

It was the knife she'd dreamed about. Sarah couldn't take her eyes off it.

"Sarah?"

She looked up and realized Matt was talking to her. "Yes?"

"Are you okay?"

Sarah nodded. "Why do you ask?"

Matt held the knife up. "It's just the way you're staring at this thing."

"Could I see it?" Sarah asked.

"Uh, sure." Matt gave her the knife, handle first.

The knife felt heavy in her hand. The handle was made of green plastic. Sarah touched the blade lightly with her thumb. It felt very sharp. As she balanced the knife in her hand, she imagined plunging it into Matt's chest. Suddenly it wasn't just a wild fantasy, but an urge growing stronger every second. She had to fight herself to keep from doing it.

"Wow," Matt said, reaching again for the knife. "You're not usually into stuff like this."

As Sarah looked at his outstretched hand, wild thoughts raced through her head. She imagined stabbing him in the neck, or sliding the knife down and chopping off his wrist. It would be so easy. It was so tempting.

*What in the world was going on?* She never had thoughts like this.

"Can I have it back?" Matt asked.

It took all her will to hand the knife back to him. Matt took it and gave her a strange look. "I don't know what's with you, Sarah. But you're really acting weird tonight," he said.

# Chapter 16

They ate by candlelight at a heavy wooden table in the dining room. Sebastian had broiled the trout, cooked potatoes, and made a salad. He sat at the head of the table, the candlelight glinting off his silver rings and bracelets.

"This is really good," Adam said between mouthfuls.

"See?" Jodie nudged him playfully. "You got to eat freshly caught fish after all."

"Except I didn't catch them," Adam said. He turned to Sebastian. "Where do you fish around here?"

"Lake Arcadia, out behind the spa," the gray-haired man replied. "Usually you can see it, but not these days, because of all the fog and rain."

"So what's the story with this place, anyway?" Matt asked. "I mean, what's it doing out here in the middle of nowhere?"

"That depends on your perspective," Sebastian replied with a smile. "You might call it the middle of nowhere, but someone else might think it's the center of everything."

Matt rolled his eyes. "Okay, then, what's it just doing here?"

Sebastian put down his fork and dabbed his lips with his napkin. "The Arcadia was built in the nineteen twenties by a millionaire named Welsh, who used it as a summer getaway for his family. Unfortunately the Depression came along soon after that, and Mr. Welsh lost everything and was forced to sell the place. The next owners turned it into an inn, but they couldn't make a go of it, so they sold it too. And after that, it kept changing hands as different owners tried to make it profitable without success. Finally, in the sixties it was pretty much taken over by hippies who used it as a commune." Sebastian smiled. "Back in the days of peace and love."

"What happened next?" Sarah asked.

"It was left abandoned until the present owner bought it," Sebastian said. "As you can see, he's spent a lot of bread fixing it up. He plans to open it on Memorial Day."

"So, who's this new owner?" Jodie asked.

"A man who prefers to remain anonymous," Sebastian replied.

Something was troubling Sarah. "It sounds

like it was left abandoned for at least twenty years. Why so long?"

Sebastian leveled his gaze at her. "In 1969, there was a murder here. A pretty gruesome one. After that, no one wanted to stick around."

"Did they think it was haunted or something?" Matt asked eagerly.

Sebastian still hadn't taken his eyes off Sarah. "Some people say it still is."

"What happened?" Jodie asked.

"Some hippie girl went on a rampage and hacked up three of her friends with an army knife," Sebastian said.

Suddenly Sarah realized Matt was staring at her. His lips began to move and she was sure he silently mouthed the words: "army knife."

Sarah felt goose bumps race up her arms, and she looked away.

"Why'd she do it?" Adam asked.

"No one really knows," Sebastian said. "Some people said she did it because her boyfriend was fooling around with another girl. Some people said it was because she wanted the other girl's boyfriend for herself, but he wasn't interested, and she just went berserk and killed them all. Maybe she just thought if she couldn't have him, no one else could, either. They tried to plead insanity at her trial, arguing that all the drugs she'd taken made her go crazy. But the jury didn't go for it."

"So what happened?" Adam asked.

"She was executed," Sebastian said. "It took years with all the appeals and stays of execution, but I've never forgotten the date. She was executed on March nineteenth, 1977."

Sarah looked up, stunned. Once again, her eyes met Matt's.

"The day you were born," he said.

# Chapter 17

Everyone at the table was silent. Sarah had her head down, but she could tell they were all staring at her. Did they think there was some connection? *Did she think there was?*

"Strange coincidence," Adam said, breaking the silence. Sarah looked up, and Adam gave her a reassuring smile.

"I'll say," Jodie agreed with a vigorous nod.

"What did this girl look like?" Matt asked Sebastian.

The gray-haired man shrugged. "Couldn't tell you."

The table grew quiet again. Sarah was hoping they'd change the subject, but Matt had one last question.

"Let me ask you something, Sebastian," he said. "Did they find the murder weapon?"

Sarah could see that Sebastian was surprised

by the question. "Why do you ask?"

"Just curious," Matt said.

"Actually, they never did," Sebastian said.

Once again, Matt stared at Sarah, this time making his eyes go wide.

"Then how did they know she killed them?" Jodie asked.

"Well, everyone knew she carried the knife," Sebastian replied. "Plus, she gave the police a confession. But you know what? That was a long time ago. I'm sure there are other things we could talk about."

Adam, Matt, and Sebastian talked about the lake and fishing for the rest of the meal. Then Sebastian pushed his chair back and got up.

"Time to pack it in," he said.

Sarah and the others looked uncertainly at one another.

"You folks can take your time," Sebastian said. "Just remember to blow the candles out when you're done."

"Well, uh, thanks for dinner," Adam said.

"You're most welcome," Sebastian said, once again staring right at Sarah.

They waited until Sebastian left, then Matt turned to the others. "You want to see something incredible?" he whispered urgently, reaching down below the table. A second later, he brought out the green knife in its sheath.

"So?" Adam looked puzzled. "It's a knife."

"It's *the* knife," Matt whispered. "The one that hippie girl killed her friends with."

"Oh, sure." Adam nodded dubiously. "Yeah, right. After more than twenty years you suddenly find it."

"I did," Matt insisted. "In the woodpile next to the fireplace. It was pushed under a log."

"Oh, my God!" Jodie gasped.

"Hey, wait a minute," Adam said. "Just because you found it in the woodpile, doesn't mean it's the one she used to kill them."

"Of course," Matt said. "There are probably a couple of dozen army knives just lying around this place."

"You're both right," Jodie said. "It might not be the actual knife, but, then again, it might."

Matt waved the knife slowly through the air, making weird *Twilight Zone* sounds.

"Stop it, Matt," Jodie said. "It's not funny. Maybe we should tell the police."

"Why bother?" Matt asked. "The murderer's already been executed. It's not like they need this now."

"What are you going to do with it?" Adam asked.

"What do you think?" Matt asked. "I'm gonna keep it, of course. This is the best souvenir I've ever found."

After dinner they moved into the lobby,

where Adam and Matt built a fire in the big stone hearth. Matt had slipped his belt through the knife sheath, and now wore the knife at his waist. For some strange reason, Sarah found she was having a difficult time not staring at it.

"I repeat what I said before," Matt said as he lit some balled-up newspaper under the kindling and logs. "That Sebastian is one tweaked guy."

"I actually thought he was pretty nice," Jodie said.

"Well, I don't like the way he stares at Sarah," Matt said.

"I noticed that too," Jodie said, turning to Sarah. "Think he has the hots for you?"

"Gross." Sarah shivered at the thought. "I hope not."

Matt struck a match, and the fire quickly roared to life. For a while they just sat and stared at the flames and felt the comforting heat radiate toward them. Adam joined the girls on the couch, but Matt stood near the hearth, poking at the logs with an iron poker.

"Okay," Matt said. "What's next?"

Sarah glanced at the others. If she had to stay in this place another night, she was perfectly happy to sit by the fire.

"Come on," Matt said. "Let's do something. This is really boring."

"I've done enough for one day," Jodie said. "You sat and watched television all day, but

Adam and I were out there for hours looking for your car."

Matt turned to Sarah. "Want to go in the hot tub?"

"I didn't bring anything to swim in," Sarah said.

"So?" Matt grinned.

"So forget it," Sarah said, taking a quick glance at Adam.

Matt put down the poker. "Well, I'm going to check it out. If anyone wants to join me, you'll know where I'll be."

"You're going alone?" Jodie asked nervously.

"Sure." Matt quickly reached to his side, and drew the army knife out of its sheath. "Anyone wants to mess with me, they're going to be in big trouble."

He left.

"This might be a good time do some more reading," Jodie said, getting up. "I've still got three hundred pages to finish. You want to go back to the room, Sarah?"

Sarah was about to say yes when Adam caught her eye. "Uh, you go ahead," she said. "I'll catch up in a little while."

Jodie looked from Sarah to Adam and back. "Okay, I'll leave you two here." Then she winked. "But only because I trust you."

She left. Sarah stared uncomfortably at the fire. Alone with Adam, she could feel a desire inside her start to glow like the coals beneath the flames, but Jodie's words echoed in her ears and made her feel guilty.

The burning wood crackled, and a log broke in two, sending up a shower of sparks. Adam got up and threw another log on, then stood near the hearth and watched it ignite. From the couch, Sarah watched the light and shadows dance on his face. *Love . . . jealousy . . . need.* The desire inside her continued to grow, while Jodie's words gradually faded.

Finally, Adam turned and looked at her.

"About the other night, Sarah," he said.

"You don't have to talk about it," Sarah said.

"I want to." He paused and stared back at the flames. "I've been thinking about it a lot, and I don't want you to get the wrong idea. I really like Jodie, and I'd never do anything to hurt her."

That wasn't what Sarah wanted to hear, but she nodded.

"Maybe if I'd met you first, it would have been different," Adam said. "But I'm going with Jodie, and that's the way things are. You're different than she is. I guess I like both of you."

It was as if he were speaking about the way Sarah used to feel for him and Matt. But that was before she and Adam had kissed. And it was before they had come here.

"I guess what I'm trying to say is that sometimes stuff happens," Adam said. "It's no one's fault, and no one's to blame. And I—I hope we can still be friends."

*Friends?* No, they could never be friends now. Sarah knew what Adam had felt when they were parked outside her house, and what he'd felt that afternoon in the woods when he'd held her in his arms. It wasn't friendship. But she also knew that he had to be feeling guilty about Matt and Jodie.

*If only Matt and Jodie weren't there.*

Somehow, she had to remind Adam of what he felt for her. "Adam, are you sure you didn't see that school bus last night?"

"What?" Adam looked surprised that she'd changed the topic. "Uh, yeah, Sarah, I'm positive."

"And what makes you think the person you saw in the woods today was me?" she asked.

Adam smiled. "Three things. The first thing was that she had red hair just like yours. The second was that she was running. The third and most important was that I caught you."

"That's for sure," Sarah said. She knew he had to be recalling that moment when he'd held her in his arms. She thought she could almost see it in his face.

Adam left the fire and sat down on the couch a few feet from her. "Look, Sarah, I know what you're thinking, and I'm really sorry if I led you on. But I . . . I didn't mean to."

"You didn't mean to kiss me?" Sarah asked innocently.

"Well, I—" Adam stammered. Sarah could see the indecision and confusion in his face. She slid a little closer and placed her hand on his.

"I think you did mean to kiss me," she said in a low voice.

He'd been staring down at her hand atop his, but now he looked up, back into her eyes. "That's not the way I remember it," he said. "The way I remember it, you kissed me."

Sarah nodded slowly. "You didn't exactly run away."

Adam turned away and stared at the crackling fire. She watched him heave a long sigh. *Love . . . jealousy . . . need.* The sensations she felt inside burned almost as brightly as the flames in the hearth. She couldn't worry about Jodie and Matt now. Only Adam mattered. She had to have him. He had to be all hers.

She slid closer. Now her knee pressed against his, and their faces were only a foot apart. "And this afternoon," she said, "when we were in each other's arms. You weren't in a rush to let go."

Adam nodded and stared down at the floor. "Not until Jodie . . ."

"Forget Jodie," Sarah whispered.

Adam's head shot up. "How can you say that, Sarah? She's my girlfriend."

"Is that what you really want?" Sarah asked.

Adam shrugged. "I don't know what I want. All I know is, that's the way things are. How could I ever break up with her?"

"The same way she broke up with Matt," Sarah replied. "They're still friends."

"Yeah, but that was different," Adam said.

"How?" Sarah asked, sliding closer. She wanted to feel his arms around her and feel his lips on hers. She reached forward and caressed his shoulder and the side of his face with her fingers. He was so handsome and thoughtful. Everything Matt wasn't.

Adam took her hand away from his face. "Look, Sarah, even if I broke up with Jodie, I couldn't do it to Matt. I mean, it would be the second time I wound up with his girlfriend."

Sarah slid closer. "It's not your problem."

The next thing she knew, she was sliding even closer, trying to put her arms around him and pull herself against him. For a moment, Adam seemed willing to go into an embrace, but suddenly he put his hands on her shoulders and gently but firmly pushed her away.

"Wow, Sarah, you've really changed," he said.

"No," Sarah said, pressing against his hands. "I've always felt this way. From the second I met you, I knew I'd made a mistake by getting involved with Matt."

"Are you serious?" Adam looked shocked.

Sarah felt herself nod.

"Well, I never knew that," Adam said. "And anyway, you don't have to be so aggressive about it."

*Aggressive?* The word hit Sarah like a slap. It

was so unlike her. She'd never been the aggressive type. Even if she wanted something terribly, she would rather go without it than act too pushy. Suddenly she realized Adam was right. She had been acting extremely aggressive. It was almost as if she'd been under some kind of spell.

To her dismay, Adam stood up. "It's as if ever since you got here, you've been a different person."

Sarah didn't know how to answer. Adam took a step. He was going to leave.

"Wait," Sarah said. Adam stopped and looked back at her with a questioning look.

"Maybe you're right," Sarah quickly said. "I don't know why I said those things. Promise me you won't tell Jodie or Matt. Please?"

Adam paused for a moment, then nodded. "Okay, Sarah. Let's just forget about it."

Sarah felt a wave of relief wash through her. Her eyes followed Adam as he walked across the lobby and disappeared down the corridor toward their rooms. Then she turned and looked back at the flames dancing in the stone hearth.

Maybe she had been too aggressive, but her feelings for him still had not changed. And neither, she suspected, had his feelings for her. She'd just come on a little too strongly, and that had scared him.

For the moment . . .

*If only Jodie and Matt weren't there.*

# Chapter 18

*Oh, wow!* Matt thought as millions of tiny bubbles billowed up around him in the hot tub. He'd had no idea that the small amount of shampoo he'd used on his hair would create so much foam. But the swirling jets of water in the tub had whipped it up into a huge frothing mountain of bubbles.

*Hey, I could get used to this*, he thought as he relaxed shoulder-deep in the hot water.

Suddenly Matt felt a draft of cool air. The steamed-up glass door to the hot-tub room opened. The air in the room suddenly turned foggy as cool, damp air from outside rushed in. From his viewpoint behind the bubbles, Matt could see only red curly hair.

"Hey, Sarah!" Matt said. "I'm glad you changed your mind. Come on in, the water's great."

She closed the door behind her and walked into the women's locker room.

*All right!* Matt thought. He was psyched that Sarah decided to join him in the hot tub.

A few moments later, the door to the women's room opened and Sarah came out. The air in the room was still so misty, he couldn't see her clearly, but who else had curly, bright-red hair? It looked like she was wearing a white T-shirt and cut-off blue jeans. She was tucking her hair into a woman's old-fashioned white rubber bathing cap.

"Hey, where'd you get the shorts?" Matt asked. "I thought you said you didn't bring anything you could swim in. And what's with the bathing cap?"

Sarah just smiled at him and finished tucking her red hair under the cap. Instead of coming toward the tub, she walked to the metal box marked "Controls" and opened it. Matt saw her hand turn up the dial that controlled the temperature.

"Hey, don't turn it up too high," Matt said with a laugh. "I don't want to get cooked."

Matt watched Sarah turn toward him and smile again. Already he could feel the water growing hotter. Matt frowned. There was something about her that looked a little different, but he couldn't quite figure out what it was. Her mouth? Her eyes? She sat down on the edge of the hot tub across from him, and put her feet in the water.

"So what did you tell Adam and Jodie?" he asked.

Sarah didn't answer him. She just slipped into

the hot tub. Her shoulders disappeared under the foaming bubbles, then her neck, then her chin. A moment later, all Matt could see was the top of her bathing cap. Then that disappeared under the bubbles too.

*Totally weird*, he thought. *What's she doing?* The water was growing so hot that sweat broke out on his forehead. He was starting to feel uncomfortable. Sarah must have turned the water temperature up all the way. And where was she, anyway?

The next thing Matt knew, he felt two hands on his thighs.

*Oh, wow!* he thought. Sarah had never done anything like this before. The water was really turning unbearably hot, but there was no way Matt was going to get out now. Not with Sarah's hands on him.

He felt her hands run down over his thighs, and knees, and down his calves. Now they closed around his ankles. Matt grinned and wiped the sweat off his forehead with a wet, sudsy hand. He didn't quite know what Sarah was up to, but he wasn't going to stop her.

Gradually, the hands closed around his ankles. Matt leaned back a little in the water, wondering what Sarah would do next.

Suddenly he felt the hands tug downward. Matt slid a little farther down in the hot water.

"Hey," he said. The hands tugged again, and

Matt felt himself being pulled a little deeper into the burning hot water. Obviously Sarah had decided to play a trick on him.

"Hey! Okay, I get the joke," he said. "Very funny. You can let go now."

But Sarah didn't let go. Instead, she tugged down again. Matt's shoulders were underwater now. It seemed like she'd been under the surface for an awful long time. Didn't she have to come up for air?

"Hey, Sarah," he shouted. "I don't want you to drown or anything."

There was another tug. Matt was worried. Sarah had been under the water much too long, and the water was much too hot. Something very weird was happening.

"Sarah!" Matt shouted. He tried to kick free, but her grip on his ankles was unbreakable. Another tug. Matt grabbed for the edge of the hot tub, but he couldn't get a good grip. Something crazy was going on. Sarah should have drowned by now.

Another tug.

"Hey, cut it out!" Matt started to kick as hard as he could, but the hands stayed around his ankles.

Another tug.

"*Help!*" he screamed. The water had turned scalding, and Sarah had pulled him down until his chin touched the surface.

"Sarah! Stop!"

Another tug. The burning hot water hit his lower lip. Matt started splashing frantically.

"*Help!*" he cried. "*Let me go!*"

Another tug.

The water went over his mouth. Matt craned his neck to keep his nose out of the water as he struggled to take one more breath.

Another tug. A moment later he disappeared under the bubbles.

# Chapter 19

*Knock, knock, knock!*

Sarah had just fallen asleep when she heard the knock on the door. She turned on the reading light next to her bed. In the other bed, Jodie stared back at her.

"Jodie? Sarah?" It was Adam.

"Just a second." Sarah got out of bed and opened the door.

Adam stood in the doorway with a worried look on his face. "Have you seen Matt?"

"No. Didn't he come back from the hot tub?"

Adam shook his head. "I guess I'd better go check in the spa." He looked away down the hall, but Sarah could see that he was hesitating. Maybe he wanted her to come. Maybe it was just an excuse for them to be alone again.

"Wait," she said. "I'll go with you."

"Hey," said Jodie. "You're not leaving me here alone."

"Give us a second," Sarah told Adam and closed the door.

The two girls quickly jumped out of bed. Sarah kneeled down beside her pack and reached inside for a pair of clean socks. Suddenly her hand touched something hard, flat, and long. Puzzled, she began to pull it out, but then stopped. She reached down and felt the plastic handle. *The knife!* The last she knew Matt had had it. What was it doing in her backpack?

Sarah glanced across the room at Jodie, who was pulling on her jeans. Could she have gotten it from Matt and put it in Sarah's pack? It didn't seem possible. Sarah was just about to ask her, when something told her not to. Instead she reached deeper into the backpack, still searching for the socks.

Now her hand felt something wet.

*What in the world . . . ?* Not wanting her other clothes to get wet, she quickly pulled it out and found herself staring at a drenched white T-shirt. Sarah quickly reached into her backpack again. This time she pulled out a pair of wet cut-off blue jeans.

"Where'd you get those?"

Sarah spun around and saw that Jodie was staring at the clothes. "I . . . I don't know."

"I know you didn't pack a T-shirt and shorts," Jodie said. "And how come they're wet?"

"I really don't have a clue," Sarah replied.

"You didn't put them in my pack, did you?"

"No way," Jodie said. "I've never seen them before."

"You think one of the guys snuck in?" Sarah asked.

"It would be a pretty good trick," Jodie said. "I know I locked the door."

Was it one of Matt's jokes? Sarah wondered. She still suspected he had a key to the room.

There was another knock on the door. "You guys almost ready?" Adam called from the hallway.

"Look, let's worry about it later," Jodie said, pulling her tennis shoes on. "Adam's waiting."

They left the room, and together with Adam, walked quickly down the hall toward the spa.

They pushed through the door into the pool area. Down at the end of the pool, they could see the glassed-in area where the hot tub was. The glass was fogged.

They went down and pushed open the door. A cloud of hot, foggy steam escaped.

"Wow, it's hot in there," Jodie said.

They could hear the water jets rumbling. A layer of bubbly foam covered the slowly churning surface of the hot tub.

"He's not in here," Adam said, letting the door close. "Let me try the men's locker room."

"I'll check the women's room," Jodie said.

Adam scowled. "What would he be doing in there?"

"There's no one else staying here," Jodie explained. "And you know Matt's sense of humor."

Sarah waited beside the hot tub while Adam and Jodie checked inside the locker rooms. Suddenly she noticed something lying in the corner. It looked like a woman's old-fashioned bathing cap. Curious, she walked over and picked it up. A second later, she felt her eyes go wide. Inside were several strands of curly red hair!

The door to the women's locker room began to open. Sarah quickly tossed the cap into the hot tub, where it disappeared under the foamy surface. But she felt deeply rattled. First she'd found the knife and wet clothes in her backpack. Now the bathing cap with the red hair. How was it possible?

"Sarah?"

"Huh?" Sarah looked up and found Jodie staring at her.

"Are you okay?" Jodie asked. "You have a really weird expression on your face."

"It must be the air in here," Sarah said quickly. "I'll be okay as soon as we get out."

A minute later Adam came out of the men's locker room, shaking his head.

"No sign of him."

They checked the weight room and the squash court before heading back down the corridor to the inn, where they checked the television room and the video-game room. Matt was nowhere to be found.

"What do you think?" Jodie asked Sarah.

Sarah was still wondering about the knife, wet clothes, and hair in the bathing cap. It simply didn't make sense. There was no way it could make sense!

"Sarah?" Jodie said. "I asked what you thought about Matt."

"Knowing Matt, this is probably another one of his practical jokes," she said. "At least, I hope it is."

Jodie turned to Adam. "You don't think anything bad happened, do you?"

Adam shrugged. "Who knows?"

"That's not the answer you're supposed to give, Adam," Jodie said impatiently. "You're supposed to say, 'Of course not, why should something bad have happened to Matt?'"

Adam smiled weakly at her. "Sorry, I keep forgetting my lines."

"Where do we look now?" Sarah asked.

They were standing in the middle of the hall. Adam turned and tried the door to room twenty-seven.

"I really have no idea where to begin looking," Adam said, pulling the door open and reaching in to flick on the light. Inside the room were a bed and dressers identical to the ones in the rooms in which they were staying. Adam backed out and closed the door.

"He could be in any one of these rooms,"

Adam said, pointing to the doorways that lined the hall. "None of the rooms is locked. There are probably a hundred rooms in this place. He could have walked into any one of them and gone to sleep."

"What do you want to do?" Jodie asked.

"Maybe we should just go to sleep," Sarah said. "I'm pretty sure this is just another one of his jokes, and he's going to show up in the morning."

"Let's hope so," Adam muttered.

Back in the room, Sarah locked the door and put the security chain on. Lying in bed, she had trouble falling asleep. It had started to rain hard again, so hard that the rain made a racket against the windows. But what really kept her awake was wondering about all the strange things that were going on.

Matt's disappearance was the least of them. He was always playing jokes like this. And as for his car, they could explain that by saying it had probably been towed to the garage. But how did you explain all the other things? The knife and wet clothes in her pack, the bathing cap with the red hairs, the school bus, her knowing the name Arcadia, dreaming about the clearing and then finding it, knowing about the diving rock? And what about Adam and Jodie and Matt all claiming they saw her in places where she was sure she hadn't been? And what about the door she was certain she'd locked? Could all of those things have been mistakes and coincidences?

The bathing cap, wet clothes, and knife bothered her the most. Matt had taken the knife with him to the hot tub. The hair in the bathing cap indicated that someone with hair like hers had been there too. And what about the wet clothes? Had someone worn them into the tub?

Was there someone around there who was pretending to be her?

"Sarah?" Jodie's voice broke the silent dark.

"Yes?"

"What are you thinking about?"

"What a strange place this is," Sarah replied.

"You're telling me," Jodie said. "Even Adam's uncle's cabin in the woods is starting to sound better than this place."

At the mention of Adam's name, Sarah felt her feelings begin to stir.

*If only Jodie and Matt weren't there. . . .*

Why did she keep thinking that?

"You still there?" Jodie asked.

"Sorry," Sarah said.

"You know what I'm thinking?" Jodie asked. "As soon as we find Matt and get his car back, I want to get out of here and never look back."

It was after three A.M. when Sarah finally fell asleep. She dreamed she was back in the clearing again, sitting cross-legged on the grass with a small circle of people. Doug, the boy with the thick blond bangs, was sitting near her. The girl named Ellen, who had dirty blond hair parted in the middle, was sitting next to Doug. A few feet away sat Mike, wearing jeans and his rawhide vest, but no shirt. Mike was playing the beautiful red wooden guitar with his eyes closed, lost in the music. The rest of them were listening. Sarah found the music monotonous and dull.

Sarah couldn't stop staring at Doug. She felt entranced by his shaggy blond hair and boyish good looks. An intense longing grew inside her. Suddenly Doug looked over at her and caught her eye. He smiled, but Sarah quickly looked away.

A few moments later, Sarah watched Doug slide his arm around Ellen's waist and pull her close. He whispered something in her ear, and then kissed her on the earlobe and got up. Sarah watched him walk away into the woods. She wished she could get up and follow him, but something was stopping her. A few moments later, Ellen rose to her feet, then crossed the clearing and entered the woods.

Sarah knew that Ellen was going to meet Doug. Her insides were churning with mixed emotions. *Love . . . jealousy . . . need.* But mostly she felt frustration that she had to sit there and listen to the dull, monotonous music.

Mike never opened his eyes or stopped playing

the guitar. But Sarah no longer watched him, or even heard what he was playing. Instead she stared at the spots where Doug and Ellen had entered the woods. She wanted Doug.

She had to have him. . . .

# Chapter 20

When Matt still hadn't returned the next morning, they decided to split up and search for him. They were starting to wonder if this was another one of his practical jokes, after all. He'd been gone an awfully long time. But maybe he was just hiding somewhere, trying to scare them.

Jodie said she'd search the parts of the spa they hadn't covered the night before. Even though it was pouring rain outside, Adam said he'd go out and cover the grounds. Sarah said she'd stay and search the inn, even if it meant looking in every empty room.

She had just finished searching the first floor of her wing and was entering the lobby when she noticed that Sebastian was setting up a tall ladder near the hearth. Next to him on the floor, a yellow plastic bucket was catching drops falling from the tiles in the ceiling.

"Good morning, Sarah," he said. "Did you sleep well?"

"Okay, I guess," Sarah replied, a little nervous about being alone with him.

Sebastian nodded slowly, gazing at her. There was something unnerving about the way he looked at her. "Where are the rest of your friends?"

"Well, Matt's disappeared, and we're trying to find him."

"Disappeared, you said?" Sebastian's bushy gray eyebrows dipped into a scowl.

"Well, he likes to play jokes," Sarah explained. "He's probably just hiding somewhere. You haven't seen him, have you?"

Sebastian rubbed his gristled chin. "Matt . . . which one was he?"

Sarah described him.

"Oh, yeah." Sebastian shook his head. "Nope, haven't seen him. But he's sure to show up. Not many places he could go, especially in weather like this."

He positioned the ladder right next to the leak in the ceiling. Sarah watched him start to climb up the ladder. She should have continued her search for Matt, but something was stopping her.

"Can I ask you a question?" Sarah asked.

"Sure."

"If you've locked the door from the inside of your room, is there any way someone could open it from the outside without using a key?"

Sebastian shook his head. "None that I know of."

That, like so many other things that were happening at the New Arcadia, was truly puzzling. She watched as Sebastian continued up the ladder.

"I bet the owner must be mad that his ceiling is leaking after all the work he's had done on this place," Sarah said.

"Oh, I don't think he cares all that much," Sebastian replied. "As long as I get it fixed, that is."

"What are you going to do?" she asked.

"Up here?" Sebastian said. He climbed the rest of the way up the ladder and started to push on one of the square white tiles. "Well, I've got to get up to the original ceiling and see where the leak's coming from."

"That's not the original ceiling?" Sarah asked.

"These tiles? Nope. This is just a subceiling. There's another whole ceiling up above it. One of the previous owners had it covered over." Sebastian pushed several of the tiles up, freeing them from the metal frame that held them in position.

"Can I see the original ceiling?" Sarah asked.

"Huh? Oh, I guess, if you want." Sebastian climbed down the ladder. "Just be careful you don't fall off."

Sarah climbed up the ladder and stuck her head through the space where Sebastian had removed the white tile. She looked up and found herself staring at a large ceiling of stained glass.

It was the ceiling she'd imagined the day before, when Matt had tested her.

*I was right!* she thought. But how in the world had she known about the ceiling?

"You see what you needed to see?" Sebastian asked after she had climbed back down.

Sarah nodded. There was something about the way he spoke to her. Like he already knew things she was just finding out.

"How long has that ceiling been covered?" she asked.

"Beats me," Sebastian said. "For as long as I've been here, that's for sure."

"How long has that been?"

Sebastian rubbed his chin. "Well, let's see, I'd say almost forever."

Sarah felt a chill. "More than sixteen years?"

Sebastian closed one eye and stared up at the ceiling with the other as he thought. "Oh, sure, plenty more than that."

Sarah took a step back, recoiling at his words. If he was telling her the truth, then the ceiling had been covered since before she was born!

*What in the world was going on?*

Feeling strangely light-headed, Sarah walked quickly back down the hall. She wanted to find Adam. She wasn't certain why, but she just wanted to be with him. She had to get back to her room, put on her jacket, and go outside to find him.

She passed the television room and paused for a second to see if Matt was in there. He wasn't. She was just about to leave when the television suddenly crackled on. Sarah froze. There was no one in there. How had it turned on?

A picture appeared on the television screen. Something inside Sarah told her she didn't want to see it. She turned to go, but then out of the corner of her eye, she saw something that made her stop. A Frisbee sailed across the television screen, and a small black-and-white dog, with a red bandanna around its neck, leaped up and caught it.

Sarah stood at the entrance to the room, mesmerized by what she was seeing. The picture on the screen changed. Sarah recognized it immediately. It was the clearing. The one she'd seen in her dreams and outside the inn. How could it possibly be on the television?

This was impossible.

But she couldn't take her eyes off the screen.

There were people in the clearing, dressed in tie-dyed T-shirts and buckskin jackets with fringes . . . the same people she'd seen in her dream.

What were they doing on television?

Who had turned the television on, anyway?

A bare-skinned boy with blond hair came on the screen, but Sarah could see only his tanned back and a few strands of love beads around his neck. He was walking across the clearing and then down a path through the woods.

Doug . . .

Sarah found herself walking toward the television, almost as if she were following him.

He turned back and smiled at her. His long blond bangs fell down over his forehead. Then he turned away and kept going. *Love . . . jealousy . . . need.* Suddenly Sarah felt like she would have stepped right through the television screen to be with him if she could.

Sarah stopped in front of the television.

Doug kept walking. The path he was on looked familiar. Soon it began to follow a small brook.

*He's going to the pool*, Sarah thought.

And then Doug was there, at the pool. "Hey, Mike," he said in a voice that was eerily familiar.

The picture on the television shifted to the boy with the beautiful red guitar, who was now sitting on the diving rock, his chest bare as he strummed a song. He paused for a moment to wave back to Doug, then closed his eyes and started strumming again.

It was that same dull, monotonous music. Sarah reached forward and pushed the channel selector. The channel flipped, but the picture remained the same. She moved the volume control up and down, but the sound of Mike's guitar remained unchanged.

On the screen now, someone was coming out of the woods near Mike. It was Ellen, the girl with the long, dirty blond hair parted in the middle. She was wearing a yellow bikini top and cutoff blue jeans.

"Hey, Ellen," Doug called. "Seen Sharon anywhere?"

Ellen pointed at the pool.

The picture shifted to the pool. Through the clear water, Sarah recognized someone swimming beneath the surface—a girl, wearing a white T-shirt tied around her waist and cut-off jeans. Her head broke the surface, a head of unmistakable red hair, which was hanging in long, loose, wet rings down over her shoulders.

She stood up in the water, her back to the screen.

From the edge of the pool, Doug waved. "Hey, Sharon!"

As she turned, she shook out her hair and ran her fingers through it. Sarah realized the white T-shirt and shorts she wore were identical to the ones she'd found in her backpack.

The person on the screen kept turning. And then Sarah was looking at someone . . . who looked just like her.

# Chapter 21

She was running. She didn't know where, but she had to get away. Away from that television, away from that inn. She burst through a door and out into the pouring rain.

*Who is Sharon? Why does she look so much like me? How could I have dreamed the same thing I saw on the television?*

*Why did everything around here seem so familiar?*

She was running along the edge of the woods. The rain splashed against her face and started to soak through the shoulders of her sweater. It was seeping into her running shoes, but she didn't care. She had to get away.

"Sarah!"

A man's voice. She didn't recognize it. Was he after her?

"Sarah, stop! Come back!"

She turned to see who was calling, and in the

same instant ran into something hard.

*Thunk!*

Everything went black.

Sarah was sitting in a hard, uncomfortable wooden chair. She tried to move her legs and arms, but her ankles and wrists were restrained by thick leather straps attached to the chair. The straps had buckles on them, like belts. No matter how hard she struggled against the straps, she couldn't get free.

A draft ran across the back of her neck. Her hair had been shaved off, and her head was under something that felt like a metallic hat.

The room was bare and empty, the walls were made of gray, unpainted cinder blocks. On the wall was the type of calendar whose pages you tore off as each day passed. The date was March 19, 1977. Across the room was a door with a single round window in it. As she watched, the grim face of a man appeared in the window. He was wearing a white collar around a dark shirt, like a priest, and crossing himself.

"The governor has refused the last-minute stay of execution," a voice said. "Do you have any final requests?"

"*Ahhh!*"

"It's okay, Sarah, it's okay." A pair of hands restrained her. Sarah realized she was lying on a bed.

She opened her eyes and looked up to see Jodie sitting beside her. Adam was sitting at the foot of the bed. Sebastian was standing near the doorway.

"Where am I?" Sarah gasped, propping herself up on her elbows. "What happened?"

Suddenly a spot on the side of her head began to throb. The pain was so excruciating that she had to lie back down again. Now she realized she was under a blanket, dressed in her red sweatshirt. She stared up in wonder at Jodie.

"You ran into a tree," she said.

"Hard enough to knock yourself out," Adam added.

Sarah glanced at Sebastian.

"He found you," Adam said. "I ran into him as he was carrying you back into the inn. We brought you in here."

Sarah gave Jodie an alarmed look.

"I made them leave while I got your wet clothes off," Jodie explained.

Gradually, the memory of what led up to her running into the tree came back to Sarah.

"I think we should leave," she said, trying to sit up again. "Really, I think we should go right now."

Jodie pressed her hands against Sarah's shoulders and gently pushed her back down. "Try to calm down. Everything's fine."

"No, it's not." Sarah started to shake her head, but the pain made her gasp. "Ow!"

"Now that she's awake, maybe you could give her some of that aspirin I gave you," Sebastian suggested.

"I'll get some water." Adam jumped up and went into the bathroom. Sarah heard the water run. A moment later he came out with a glass and handed it to Jodie.

Jodie put a couple of long white capsules into Sarah's hand. "Try to take these. It'll make your head feel better."

Sarah started to bring her hand toward her mouth. Then it occurred to her that the pills had come from Sebastian. She suddenly stopped and stared at them.

"They're just aspirin," Jodie reassured her. "No one's trying to slip you anything."

Sarah smiled weakly. Why was she being so untrusting? *Maybe because nothing made sense anymore.*

Sarah put the capsules in her mouth and sipped the water. The pills were hard to swallow, but she managed to get them down.

"Why don't you just lie back and relax," Jodie said. "We're here, and we're going to take care of you."

Sarah eased back into the pillow, wondering if Jodie would be so nice if she knew about her and Adam. Her head had just touched the pillow when she suddenly sat up again.

"What now?" Jodie asked.

"Matt," Sarah said. "Have you found him?"

"No," Adam said. "But Sebastian said he'd help us look."

Sarah stared at Jodie with wide eyes. "You're not going to leave me alone?"

"No way," Jodie said. "The guys will look. I'm keeping my eye on you from now on."

"Oh, okay." Sarah settled back uncomfortably. She really didn't want to be alone with Jodie, but under the circumstances, she didn't know what other choice she had.

"I guess we'd better go," Adam said, getting up. He looked back at Jodie and Sarah. "You sure you'll be okay?"

"No, but we'll make the best of it," Jodie said.

"Okay, see you later." Adam bent down and kissed Jodie on the forehead. Despite her discomfort, Sarah felt a bolt of jealousy race through her.

A moment later, Adam and Sebastian went out the door. Jodie locked the door behind them. Then she slumped down in the chair she'd pulled next to the bed. For a second Sarah and she stared into each other's eyes.

*I hate you . . .* The thought flashed into Sarah's mind. Why? she wondered. Because of Adam?

"You ran into a tree," Jodie finally said.

Sarah nodded. *The television . . . the girl who looked just like her . . . The clothes that were the same as the ones she'd found in her backpack . . .*

"Mind if I ask how?" Jodie asked.

"I don't know," Sarah said. "I was just running. I guess I didn't see it."

"I thought you were going to look for Matt in the inn," Jodie said.

"I was . . ." Sarah's words trailed off.

"You decided to take a run instead?" Jodie said.

Sarah didn't like her tone. There was something suspicious about it. "Why are you interrogating me?"

Jodie let out a deep sigh, then got up and went over to the dresser. She opened a drawer and took out the green army knife in its sheath.

"Look familiar?" she asked.

Sarah nodded.

"I found it in your backpack when I went to get the sweatshirt," Jodie said. "Mind telling me how it got there?"

"I don't know," Sarah said.

"The last time I saw it, Matt was wearing it," Jodie said. "He was going to the hot tub. I thought that was the last time any of us saw him."

"It was," Sarah said.

"Except that all of a sudden you had a wet T-shirt and shorts, and this knife," Jodie said.

"I swear, Jodie, I don't know where the T-shirt and shorts came from," Sarah said. "And the knife just appeared in my backpack. I thought you or Matt must have put it there."

"Why didn't you tell us?" Jodie asked.

"I . . . I was afraid to," Sarah said. "So many

weird things had happened. I didn't want you to blame me for them."

"Why would we blame you?" Jodie asked.

"I don't know. I was just afraid that you would."

Jodie shook her head and stared up at the ceiling. "This is the strangest trip I've ever been on."

"I know," Sarah said. "That's why I think we ought to leave right now. Before anything else bad happens."

"You think something bad has happened to Matt?" Jodie asked.

A strange, apprehensive sensation swept through Sarah. She couldn't quite explain it, except that she was suddenly quite certain that something bad *had* happened to Matt. And that somehow, she was responsible.

# Chapter 22

Sarah dozed on and off for the rest of the afternoon. Dreams came and went, almost all of them involving Doug, Ellen, Mike and the Arcadia. But it was the old Arcadia, filled with details like the stained-glass ceiling in the lobby. Sarah no longer wondered or cared how she knew about all these things. But a constant sense of dread from within warned her that if she didn't leave here soon, more bad things would happen.

Jodie sat next to a desk lamp, reading. The army knife remained on her lap. Sarah sensed that something had changed. Jodie didn't trust her anymore.

They didn't see Adam until dinnertime. When he knocked and entered the room alone, they knew he still hadn't found Matt. He slumped down into a chair and took off his hiking boots.

"I've been walking around all day," he moaned. "My feet are killing me."

Suddenly he was staring at the knife in Jodie's lap. "Where did you find that?"

"In Sarah's backpack," Jodie said. "Sarah says she has no idea how it got there."

"That true?" Adam asked, looking at Sarah.

Sarah nodded.

"More weirdness," Adam said uncomfortably.

*Imagine if they knew about the television*, Sarah thought.

"What do you think happened to Matt?" she asked.

Adam slowly shook his head. "I can't help thinking that if he was playing a joke he'd have ended it by now."

"I know," Sarah said. Her head started to throb whenever she thought about him.

"Maybe he decided to go get the car himself," Jodie said. "Like he got a ride from someone."

"Like who?" Adam asked. "And why didn't he tell us?"

They were all quiet for a moment. Sarah knew Adam was right, but she tried not to think of where that left them. None of the other possibilities was pleasant to consider.

Some were frightening.

"Has anyone seen Sebastian?" Sarah asked.

Adam looked surprised. "You mean he didn't come back here?"

Jodie shook her head.

"We split up out in the woods," Adam said.

"He said he'd stop back here and check to make sure you guys were okay."

"Great," Jodie groaned. "Now he's disappeared again."

"Maybe he went fishing for our dinner," Sarah said hopefully.

She watched as Adam and Jodie exchanged glances. Then Jodie turned to her. "Don't you hear it?"

Sarah was quiet. Suddenly she realized that the wind was howling and rain was splattering against the windows.

"It's a real storm now," Adam said. "It's been getting worse all afternoon. I seriously doubt he went fishing."

No sooner were the words out of his mouth than the lights went off.

"Adam? Jodie?" Sarah asked anxiously, staring into the dark.

"It's okay, Sarah," Adam said. "Jodie?"

"I'm still here."

"What happened?" Sarah asked.

"The power's out," Adam said. "I guess we ought to wait a few minutes. If it's a problem at the utility plant, they should get the electricity back on pretty soon. If it's a line that's down, then it's going to take a while."

They sat and waited in the dark for a few moments.

"Adam, I don't care what the problem is,"

Jodie said. "I don't like sitting here in the dark. Please do something, okay?"

"Okay, look," Adam said. "I'm going across the hall to get my flashlight. Don't go anywhere."

"I don't think we could if we wanted to," Sarah said nervously.

"Do you want the knife?" Jodie asked him in the dark.

For a second they heard nothing but the crash of thunder. Then Adam said, "No, you keep it."

They heard the door squeak as Adam opened it and went out into the hall.

"What would we do without him?" Sarah asked.

"I know," said Jodie. "He's incredibly brave. I mean, even to leave this room in the dark. Right now to get me to leave this room, I think the place would have to be on fire."

"Don't joke," Sarah said. "That could be next."

"You're right," Jodie said. "I'm really starting to get worried about Matt. Aren't you?"

"Yes," Sarah said. Matt's safety was her biggest worry, but there were a lot of others. And as impossible as it seemed, somehow she sensed that all the worries were related. Then again, it had been obvious ever since they arrived at this inn that almost anything was possible.

"Sarah?" Jodie said in the dark.

"Yes?"

"It feels better when we're talking," Jodie said.

"Like the words fill up the room or something."

"I know what you mean."

"It just seems as if everything possible is going wrong," Jodie said. "Anyway, how's your head?"

"It feels better, thanks." Sarah's thoughts started to drift back to what she'd seen on the television before. It was the oddest thing she'd ever seen.

"Sarah?" Jodie said.

"Oh, sorry, I'm supposed to keep talking."

"I hope I'm not forcing you," Jodie said.

"No, it makes me feel better too."

"Good. Doesn't it seem as if Adam's taking a long time?"

"Do you want me to go see what's going on?" Sarah asked. She started to get out of bed.

"*No!*" Jodie gasped loudly. Sarah suddenly realized that she sounded very scared.

"Maybe I should be the one asking if you're okay," Sarah asked.

"I am, but I'm scared," Jodie said. "And I really, really don't want to be left alone again in this place."

The door opened and Sarah found herself squinting into the beam of a flashlight.

"Sorry I took so long," Adam said, closing the door behind him. "It wasn't easy to find my way around in the dark."

"So now what?" Jodie asked.

"I say we go down to the office," Adam said. "There's a phone in there. Even if I have to break the door down, I think it's time we called someone."

"Sounds good to me," Jodie said.

"Me, too," said Sarah. "But I'd really like to get dressed first."

"Oops, I forgot about that," Jodie said. "Adam, can we borrow your flashlight?"

"Sure." Adam handed the flashlight to Jodie.

"I think it means you either have to close your eyes or wait in the hall," Sarah said.

"I'll close my eyes," Adam said.

Jodie shined the flashlight at Sarah and she started to get out of bed, but then Jodie turned the flashlight on Adam, who was covering his eyes with his hands. "Wait a minute. How do we know you're not peeking?"

"Boy Scout's honor," Adam said.

"You're not a Boy Scout," said Jodie. "Would you mind waiting out in the hall?"

"You guys are no fun," Adam said. Jodie kept the flashlight on him until he went out the door.

"And no peeking," Sarah said.

"Okay, okay."

The door shut. The joking quickly passed and the grim nature of the situation returned. They were stuck in the dark. Matt had disappeared. There seemed to be no way out of the inn. Sarah took the flashlight from Jodie and started to get clothes out of her pack. She selected another pair of jeans and a blue turtleneck to wear under the red sweatshirt.

"Okay," she said. "Let's go."

They went out into the dark hall and found Adam waiting there. Sarah handed the flashlight to him and they headed toward the lobby.

"If you were the caretaker here and the electricity went off and you knew people were staying in our rooms, wouldn't you come see if they were all right?" Adam asked as they walked.

"Yes," said Sarah.

"So where's Sebastian?" Jodie asked.

"I swear, I don't get it," Adam said.

They got down to the lobby. Everything was dark. Adam walked straight to the office and tried the door.

"Still locked," he said. "You guys wait here."

"Where are you going?" Jodie asked.

"Just over to the fireplace."

They watched him walk over to the stone hearth, pick up something, and return.

"Aim this at the door to the office," Adam said, handing the flashlight to Sarah.

She did as she was told, shining the flashlight at the glass-and-wood door. Adam stood beside it, and she saw that he had the iron poker in his hands. He swung the poker at the glass.

*Crash!*

The glass shattered. Adam reached inside and opened the door.

"Okay, I'll need that now," he said, reaching

for the flashlight. Sarah gave it to him, and he carefully stepped over the broken glass and went into the office. From outside the girls watched him pick up the phone.

"Darn it," he swore angrily.

"What's wrong?" Jodie asked.

Adam looked back at them in the dark with a grim expression. "Phone's dead."

# Chapter 23

In an attempt to save the batteries in the flashlight, and to get some heat, they decided to build another fire in the hearth. Adam built a pyramid of newspaper, kindling, and logs, and soon a fire was roaring and the lobby was lit with flickering orange light.

"Well, I guess we should thank Sebastian for one thing," Sarah said. "He sure supplied us with plenty of dry wood."

"That's about all we can thank him for," Jodie said sourly.

"Well, he also let us stay here," Adam said.

"I'm starting to think we would have been better off spending the night in the car," Jodie said.

"Then we would have started eating your freeze-dried food last night instead of tonight," Adam said.

"I have to say that I don't have much of an appetite right now," Sarah said.

"I know that given what's going on here, it's probably bad manners to feel hungry," Adam said, "but I happen to be starved."

"I'm kind of hungry too," Jodie admitted.

"The food's still in my pack," Sarah said.

"Okay," said Adam, "I'll go get it. You guys want to come or wait here?"

"Is there a lot of wood on the fire?" Jodie asked.

"Yeah, I don't think it'll go out for a while," Adam said.

"I guess we'll stay here, then," Jodie said. "Just don't take too long."

They watched Adam go back down the hall, carrying the flashlight.

"Could you imagine what it would be like if Adam disappeared too?" Jodie asked.

"Don't even say it," Sarah replied.

Adam returned fairly quickly with the camping food and a small cooking kit. It wasn't long before they were eating scrambled eggs. Even Sarah had some. They ate without speaking, until Sarah broke the silence.

"It's been almost twenty-four hours since we last saw Matt," she said.

"I know," Adam said.

"I just hope nothing bad happened to him," Jodie said.

"We don't know that anything happened to

him at all," Adam said. "It's better not to let our imaginations get too crazy."

"But what if something did happen?" Jodie asked.

"Look," Adam said. "For every bad thing that could have happened, something good could have happened too."

"Like what?" Sarah asked.

"Like . . . suppose Matt went up to the road for some reason, and while he was up there, a car came by and they gave him a ride into town or wherever that garage is. Except they're not finished working on the car, so he has to hang around for a while. He tries to call, but no one answers the phone in the office. Finally the car's fixed and he tries to come back to get us, but the road's washed out by the storm and he can't get through. He can't call, either, because our phone's dead."

"I don't know if that's what happened, but you've got a good imagination," Sarah said.

"Thanks, Sarah," Adam replied. But then he put down his food and stood up. "You know what? I don't believe a word of what I just said, either. I just don't get it. He said he was going to the hot tub. What could have happened?"

"Plenty," Jodie said.

"Like what?" Adam asked her.

"Who knows?" Jodie said. "Anything can happen here. We saw Sarah running through the woods, and she swore it wasn't her. We saw Matt leave with the knife, and it wound up in Sarah's pack. Did Sarah tell you about the wet clothes?"

"No." Adam scowled at Sarah. "What wet clothes?"

"I found a wet T-shirt and cut-off jeans in my pack," Sarah said. "I never saw them before."

*At least, not until the television went on. . . .* But Sarah knew she couldn't tell them about that.

"Who could have put them there?" Adam asked.

Sarah and Jodie glanced at each other and shrugged.

"This is getting totally bizarre," Adam said. He shook his head and put his hands on his hips. "Unless Sebastian's behind it somehow."

"But we hardly ever see him," Jodie said.

"I know," Adam stared down at the floor. Then suddenly, he picked up the flashlight again and turned toward the door.

"Where are you going?" Jodie asked.

"I know this is crazy, but ever since Matt disappeared, I've had this weird feeling he was still somewhere in the spa. I just want to go back and check."

"Now?" Sarah asked incredulously.

"Yeah. I promise I won't be too long."

"What about us?" Jodie asked.

"I'm sure you'll be fine. Just wait here by the fire. You know how to add logs, right?"

"It doesn't seem to take a lot of brains," Sarah said.

"Okay, see you later." Once again, they watched Adam leave. Sarah turned to Jodie and noticed that she'd clasped her hands together and shut her eyes.

"What are you doing?" she asked.

Jodie opened her eyes. "Praying he comes back."

# Chapter 24

After Adam left, Jodie and Sarah both moved to chairs closer to the fire.

"I really don't understand why he had to go look now," Jodie said.

"Because Matt's his best friend," Sarah answered. "He really hasn't stopped looking for him since we realized he'd disappeared."

"I guess you're right," Jodie said with a sigh. Even though she was sitting near the fire, she hugged herself as if she were cold. "I just want to get out of here."

Sarah nodded. She also wished Jodie would get out of there. Forever. *And leave Adam for her.*

Sarah shook her head. Where did these weird thoughts come from? It almost felt like another person was thinking them. It seemed like her mood constantly swung back and forth—from being terrified of this place to wishing she and

Adam could just be here together by themselves. She was gradually becoming aware of a change in her attitude toward the New Arcadia. Not that she loved the place, but at times she had a feeling that she belonged there somehow.

For a while she and Jodie sat quietly by the fire, listening to the wood crackle and pop as it burned. Poor Jodie, Sarah thought. Of everyone involved, she was the most innocent, the least suspecting.

"Jodie?" Sarah said.

"Yes?"

"Can I ask you a really crazy question?"

"Uh, okay."

"What would you do if you found out Adam had kissed another girl?"

Jodie stared back at her. "Why do you ask?"

"I don't know," Sarah lied. "Just to talk, I guess."

"I'd kill him, what else?" Jodie said.

"I'm serious," Sarah said.

"So am I," Jodie replied.

"Be honest," Sarah said.

"It just seems like a really strange thing to want to talk about right now," Jodie said.

"Got something better to talk about?" Sarah asked.

"Hmmm." Jodie pressed a finger against her lips. "Okay, what would I really do? Probably be really angry and upset. Oh, and I'd probably tell him that if it ever happened again, it was over between us."

Sarah nodded and gazed at the fire, absent-mindedly twisting the mood ring around her finger. Why did she care what Jodie thought? Jodie wasn't important. Sarah would never let Ellen stand between her and Doug. . . .

*Ellen . . . ? Doug . . . ?* Why had she thought of them? What did they have to do with it?

"Can I ask you a question?" Jodie said.

Sarah felt her stomach grow tight. "Uh, okay."

"Are you worried that something like that might happen with Matt?"

Sarah couldn't have cared less. All Mike wanted to do was strum boring songs on his guitar all day long.

*Mike . . . ?*

Jodie had asked about Matt, not Mike. Sarah pressed her fingers against her eyes. Why was her mind skipping around like this? Why couldn't she keep it straight anymore?

"I guess you always wonder," Sarah said.

"It's funny, but I never do," Jodie said. "Maybe it's dumb, but I don't think Adam would ever do something like that."

"But what if Adam wasn't the one doing it?" Sarah asked. "I mean, what if some other girl kissed him?"

"You mean, it was someone he didn't want to kiss?" Jodie asked. "She just sort of caught him by surprise?"

"Well, not exactly," Sarah said. "But what if there was a girl he sort of wondered about, and she wondered about him, and the kiss just sort of happened?"

"What would they be doing together, anyway?" Jodie asked.

"Maybe they were at a party," Sarah said.

Jodie picked up a small twig and threw it into the fire. They both watched it ignite and burn. "I don't know, Sarah. There are a lot of maybes and supposes here. It's getting a little hard to follow. But basically, I'd just ask him to promise me he'd never see her again."

"Okay, now let me add just one more suppose," Sarah said. "Suppose the girl was the girlfriend of Adam's best friend?"

Jodie squinted at Sarah. "You really are worried about me and Matt, aren't you?"

"Well . . ." Sarah said. She wasn't at all. But maybe it would help to mislead Jodie.

"I've always thought that must have bothered you," Jodie said. "I mean, how could it not bother you? He and I went together for nearly two years. Usually when something like that ends, you never speak to the person again. It must seem really strange to you that Matt and I stayed friends."

"Sort of," Sarah admitted.

"To tell you the truth, it seemed kind of strange to me, too," Jodie said with a smile. "But somehow we just did. He didn't even seem to mind that much when I started going with Adam. I mean, imagine that. I went from him to his best friend. I really thought it would kill him."

*Maybe it just did . . .* Sarah thought.

Just then they heard someone and turned. Adam was coming toward them. The arms and legs of his clothes were wet, and he looked very pale, even in the dim light.

"I . . . I found Matt," he gasped.

# Chapter 25

"Where is he?" Jodie asked.

Before Adam could answer, the image appeared in Sarah's mind. A reddish body floating in the hot tub . . .

"He's dead," Adam said.

Jodie gasped and brought her hand to her mouth.

"There was nothing I could do," Adam said. He sat down on the edge of the hearth, his hands clasped together, his head bowed. "He must have been in the hot tub a long time. I mean, even before he . . . And at that temperature . . ." He shook his head. "I guess we didn't see him the first time because of the foam on the surface of the water."

Jodie slid into Sarah's arms and sobbed. Strangely, Sarah felt nothing. Was it that she simply couldn't comprehend that Matt was dead?

Was she in shock? Why didn't she care?

"What made you go back and check the hot tub?" Jodie asked, wiping the tears out of her eyes with the sleeve of her blouse.

"I don't know," Adam said. He too rubbed a tear out of his eye with the palm of his hand. "I just had this weird feeling. I guess I thought of it yesterday, but it was the kind of thing that was so awful I really didn't want to go and see if it was true. Know what I mean?"

Sarah realized he was looking at her as he spoke. As if he felt bad for her. As if he was apologizing to her because Matt was her boyfriend. Sarah nodded dumbly and forced herself to think of something to say.

"Where did you leave him?" she asked.

"In the locker room." Adam shook his head, and his shoulders trembled. "I didn't know what else to do."

"Shouldn't we bury him or something?" Jodie asked.

"You mean, go outside?" Adam asked.

"Well . . ." Jodie hesitated and wiped more tears away with her hands. "At least we should call the police."

"How?" Adam asked. "The phone's dead. Sebastian's disappeared again. We can't walk out of here."

"You think Sebastian has something to do with this?" Sarah heard herself ask. But she knew it hadn't been her idea to say that. *If it wasn't her idea, whose idea was it?*

Jodie stared at her. "You mean, you think he killed Matt?"

"I think it's possible," Adam said. "The heat control was turned all the way up. I guess it's conceivable that Matt fell asleep and drowned, but in water that hot, I find it hard to believe. I mean, why didn't he just get out? I've been thinking about the wet clothes and the knife in Sarah's pack. What if Sebastian put them there to try to make us think Sarah did it?"

Sarah wondered if it was possible. But how could Sebastian make the television go on? How could the television show the same places and people she'd been dreaming about?

"Now I *really* want to get out of here," Jodie groaned.

"Not tonight," Adam said.

"Well, then first thing tomorrow morning," Jodie said. "I don't care if I have to walk all the way home. This is the last night I spend in this place."

"I think you're right, Jodie," Adam said. "We should leave first thing in the morning. But let's try to remember that we don't know what happened. It's crazy to start letting our imaginations run wild. Matt could have fainted, or had a seizure or something. We just don't know."

Jodie moved away from Sarah, then wrapped her arms around herself and shivered. "Well, I think there's something totally creepy about this place. Ever since we got here, things have been going wrong."

"They started going wrong before we got here," Adam reminded her. "Remember how we got lost? Then Sarah thought she saw that school bus, and we went off the road. All that happened before we ever set foot in this place."

Sarah crossed her arms and stared at the fire. She wondered what Adam would say if he knew what she knew . . . about locked doors that magically opened, and televisions that magically went on to show scenes of things that must have happened twenty-five years ago. Scenes that didn't change from channel to channel and had nothing to do with any television show.

How had she known all those things about the Arcadia? Who were Doug, Mike, and Ellen, and why did they figure so prominently in her dreams and on the television? And what about Sharon, who looked so much like her that they might have been doubles? Sarah didn't have the answers yet. But she had a feeling that when she found out, it would also explain Matt's death.

At least, that's what she hoped.

It was almost midnight when Adam got up to throw another log on the fire.

"I guess we'd better decide where to sleep tonight," he said.

"Sleep?" Jodie laughed bitterly. "You must be kidding me. There's no way I'm going to sleep tonight."

"Well, we still have to decide where we're going to stay," Adam said. "I figure we can either stay here by the fire or in the rooms."

"I think wherever we stay, we should all stay together," Sarah said.

Adam quickly nodded. "If we stay by the fire, we can take turns staying up and adding logs," he said. "That way one of us will always be awake while the others rest."

"But if we go in the room, we can lock the door and use the security chain," Jodie said.

"I vote for staying by the fire," Sarah said, recalling her experience with the door locks.

"Well, okay," Jodie said. "As long as we agree that each of us will really stay awake when it's our turn."

"Okay, look," Adam said. "Jodie, you seem like the least likely to sleep, so why don't you take the first shift? Uh, say until two o'clock?"

Jodie nodded. Adam glanced at Sarah. "You want to go second?"

"No, you take the second shift," Sarah told him.

"All right," Adam said. "I'll wake you up around four."

The fire crackled, and Sarah watched the sparks and smoke rise up into the star-lit sky. She was part of a group of about ten people, all sitting around the fire, staring into the dancing flames. Tonight there was no one strumming a guitar. The only sounds were the sizzling and crackling of the wood burning in the fire, and the occasional shrill call of some animal in the woods.

Only one face in the group was clear to her. The girl named Ellen was sitting across the way, wearing jeans and a long peasant blouse. Her long hair was held in place by a headband with an Indian design on it.

Soon, without a word, Ellen rose and walked off toward the woods.

After a few moments, Sarah rose and followed.

There was a full moon, filling the woods with eerie shadows. She could just see Ellen ahead of her, following a trail. She stayed behind, walking quietly, making no effort to catch up.

The path led to a wooden landing. In the moonlight, Sarah could see that they'd come to the edge of a cliff. From the landing, wooden steps cut back and forth down the face of the cliff to a dock. Beyond the dock, she could see a vast, dark lake with a long streak of milky white moonlight shimmering on its surface. The lights from a few houses on the far shore glowed in the distance, and a vast canopy of stars twinkled above.

Ellen started down the steps.

Sarah waited a few moments, and then followed.

At the bottom of the steps, Ellen walked out

on the dock to the very end and stood there with her arms crossed, staring out across the water.

Slowly, quietly, Sarah came up behind, feeling the rough wooden planks of the dock under her feet. As she walked under the moonlight, she glanced down at her mood ring. It was as black as the sky above.

When she was a dozen feet away, Ellen suddenly turned around, looking startled. "Oh, you scared me."

"Sorry."

"What . . . what are you doing here, Sharon?" Ellen seemed nervous.

"I just wanted to see the lake."

Ellen nodded. "It's weird, isn't it? About Mike. I can't believe he'd just split without telling us."

"It's kind of freaky," Sarah said.

"What do you think happened?" Ellen asked.

"I don't have a clue."

Ellen nodded and turned away to look at the lake.

Behind her, Sarah reached down and felt the smooth, plastic handle of the knife in her hand. . . .

# Chapter 26

Sarah's eyes burst open. She was lying on the couch, facing the hearth. The logs had burned down to blackened rods, and small reddish flames skipped around them as if looking for fresh wood to feed off.

On the floor beside the couch, Jodie lay with her head on a pillow, her eyes closed tightly as she slept.

Sarah sat up and yawned, then looked around. Suddenly, she felt a shiver.

Adam wasn't there.

Where was he? Had something happened to him?

She looked around with wide eyes. The rest of the lobby seemed dark and quiet, the fire no longer bright enough to light it. If the fire went out, they'd be plunged into total darkness.

Sarah quickly got up and put two new logs on the fire. Once again she looked around.

Where could Adam have gone? Why would he leave them?

It was very quiet and still. The new logs on the fire had not yet caught, so there was no crackling and sizzling.

Then Sarah thought she heard something. She held her breath, trying not to listen to the sound of the rapid beating of her heart.

Faint voices.

They seemed to be coming from the east wing.

She glanced back at Jodie. Should she wake her? No, why scare her? It might just be Adam and Sebastian talking. Sarah listened a moment more.

She decided to go down the hall and see if she could find them. As she left the lobby and entered the dark hall, she saw a faint, bluish glow down at the far end. As she walked toward it, she could hear the voices more distinctly.

It wasn't Adam and Sebastian.

It was the television.

A moment later she stepped into the television room. The large-screen television was on. But the entire inn was dark. There was no power. How could this— Sarah caught herself. Why bother asking? Things like this just happened at the New Arcadia, that's all.

She stared at the television screen. She could see the outside of the inn. See, at least, what must have been the old Arcadia. The shutters on the windows were hanging loose, and the paint was peeling off the exterior walls in large white flakes.

A crowd of people was standing around several old ambulances and police cars. The people all had long hair and sideburns, and they were wearing bell-bottoms and brightly colored T-shirts.

The front door of the Arcadia opened, and out of the shadows from inside came two ambulance attendants wearing white clothes and pushing a stretcher. On the stretcher was a long gray bag.

A body bag.

The crowd parted silently as the attendants slid the stretcher into the ambulance. Now another ambulance crew came out of the hotel pushing yet another stretcher, followed quickly by a third. Each body went into a different ambulance. Then the crews got in and drove away.

A man in a gray suit came out of the hotel and faced the crowd of onlookers. He had shorter hair and shorter sideburns than the others. He told them to pack up their things and leave. The hotel was going to be condemned.

People in the group nodded and started to turn away with surprisingly little resistance. It almost seemed as if they were eager to go.

Standing in front of the television, Sarah watched the group start to disperse. Whose bodies had been in those bags? Did they have anything to do with her dreams?

Then the door to the inn opened once again, and a policeman with a moustache stepped out.

A moment later two more policemen stepped out. Behind them followed a man in a brown suit, leading a young woman whose hands were handcuffed behind her back. Her head was bent down so that her face was not visible.

Sarah felt a cold shiver. The young woman's hair was red and curly.

As she stepped into the sunlight, the man leading her paused, waiting for a police car to pull up. The car stopped. The man in the brown suit pulled open the back passenger door and started to guide the young woman into the car. Just before she got in, she suddenly looked up.

Sarah gasped and took a step back. No, no! It wasn't possible!

"She looks just like you," a voice said.

It wasn't a voice from the television.

Sarah spun around. Behind her, Adam was standing in the doorway of the TV room. He glanced from the screen to Sarah. "What's going on, Sarah?"

"I don't know."

In the dim, bluish light of the television, Adam reached for a wall switch and flicked it. No lights went on.

"How come the television's working?" he asked.

"I don't know."

"I think you do."

"I don't, Adam. I swear."

He came closer. In the gray-blue light, Sarah

watched Adam, who was looking at her carefully. Was he looking for the knife? On the television, the man in the brown suit helped the girl with the red hair get into the back of the car. One of the police officers slammed the door.

"That girl looked just like you," Adam said.

"I know," said Sarah.

"Who is she?"

"I don't know."

Adam frowned and stepped closer to the television set. Sarah didn't know what he was going to do. On the screen, they could see the police car with the red-haired girl inside pull away from the inn, leaving the crowd behind.

"They look like hippies," he said. "What show is this?"

"It's not a show," Sarah said.

Adam frowned and changed the channel. The picture remained the same. He looked back at her.

"What's going on?" he asked.

Sarah shook her head, still stunned that the girl on the screen had looked so much like her. She saw a pattern to her dreams now—from holding the knife, to the bodies being brought out in bags, to the dream of her strapped in a chair.

An electric chair . . .

The girl they'd seen on the screen was executed on the day Sarah was born. . . .

Adam pressed the television's power switch. The picture remained on. He reached behind it and pulled the plug out of the wall.

The television was still on.

"This is too weird." Adam started to back away from the set. "I'm serious, Sarah, what's going on here?"

"I wish I could tell you," Sarah said.

"Well, what are you doing in here?"

"I woke up before," Sarah said. "You weren't around. Then I heard something, and came down here thinking it was you."

"I was in the office, trying to see if I could get the phone to work," Adam said.

That's when they heard a scream.

Adam and Sarah stared at each other.

"Jodie!" Sarah gasped.

"It came from the lobby!" Adam said. He took a step, but then stopped.

"Aren't you going to see what's wrong?" Sarah asked.

"Yes," he said. "But you're coming, too."

Sarah understood immediately. He didn't trust her. He wasn't going to let her out of his sight.

Together they ran down the hall and came out into the lobby. Jodie was standing next to the hearth with a pillow clutched to her chest, trembling.

"Are you okay?" Adam put his arm around her shoulders.

Jodie nodded, but still looked really scared. "Where were you? I woke up and I was alone."

Adam and Sarah exchanged a hasty glance. For a moment neither of them knew what to say.

"I—I went into the office to check out the phone," Adam said. "Sarah woke up and didn't see me, so she went looking. We ran into each other down the hall just a second before you screamed."

Jodie stared at him. "You're sure that's all it was?"

"Yes." Adam nodded.

Jodie's eyes met Sarah's. Sarah wondered if Jodie was thinking about the conversation they'd had earlier in the evening about jealousy.

"Really, Jodie," Sarah said. "That's all."

Jodie sat down on the edge of the couch. She was still shaking. "Well, I'd really appreciate it if you'd both stay right here for the rest of the night."

"Don't worry," Adam said. "I'm not going anywhere."

It must have been around four A.M. The three of them sat around the fire, staring at the flames. Sarah leaned against the arm of the couch and tried to avoid Adam's eyes. She was relieved that Jodie seemed to be staying awake. It meant Adam couldn't ask any questions. . . .

Especially since Sarah had no answers.

# Chapter 27

Sarah saw Doug standing alone at the top of a green wooden landing. He was wearing a pair of jeans covered with patches, and a denim work shirt. Below him were the stairs that led down the face of the cliff to the dock and the boat house. It was a sunny day, and she could see that he was gazing out over the lake. The breeze lifted his thick blond hair and made it dance. She looked down at the mood ring on her finger. It was red. As she walked toward him, she felt an incredible yearning inside—to run her fingers through his hair . . . to kiss and hold him. . . .

"Doug?"

He turned. His eyes were reddened as if he'd been crying. "Oh, hi."

"You're really upset, aren't you?" she asked.

He nodded. "I just can't believe Ellen would take off without telling me."

"Isn't it freaky?" she asked. "First Mike, and then Ellen?"

Doug seemed to wince. "You think they planned it?"

"I always had the feeling they liked each other," she said.

"Man, I don't know." Doug shook his head. "It just blows my mind."

He turned and looked back out at the lake. She stepped closer and placed her hand on his shoulder.

"But I'm still here," she said.

"Yeah, I know." Doug nodded, but didn't look at her.

"Doug?" she said softly, turning his shoulder so that he faced her.

"What?" He had a puzzled look on his face.

"I never told you this," she said. "But I always liked you more than Mike. I always wished we could be together. Now that Mike and Ellen are gone, couldn't we?"

He stared back at her. The expression on his face turned hard, and he shook his head. "No, I'm sorry, but I just don't feel that way about you."

"But you haven't let yourself—" she began.

"No!" Doug shook his head firmly.

He wouldn't even give her a chance. She felt all the love inside her turn to anger as she reached down to her waist and felt the cold, plastic knife handle. On her finger, the mood ring had turned black. Well, if she couldn't have him, no one else would either. . . .

When Sarah awoke, the lobby was filled with the dimmest gray light. It was the dawn! She couldn't believe she'd actually fallen asleep.

She looked around and saw that Jodie had also dozed off again, her head resting against Adam's thigh.

Sarah wished she could just kill her. . . .

*No! What was she thinking? What was wrong with her?* Sarah's gaze rose and met Adam's.

"Good morning," he said.

"I guess I fell asleep." She yawned.

"I guess you did."

"Did you?" she asked.

Adam shook his head. "I've been waiting for you to wake up."

"If it's because you want to ask me questions, I'm sorry, but I don't have any answers," Sarah said. "I really, really don't."

"Then why don't you tell me what you think is going on," Adam said. "Just make some wild guesses."

"I really don't want to," Sarah said.

"Why not?" Adam asked.

"Because—" Sarah began, but stopped.

"What were you going to say?" Adam asked.

"It doesn't make sense," Sarah said. "Ever since we got here, I've known about things I've never seen before. I've dreamed things that couldn't be real, and then seen them on that television. I've known about events that happened before I was born . . . things I couldn't possibly know about."

"Why didn't you tell us?" Adam asked.

"I thought you'd think I was crazy," Sarah said. "I mean, after the pink school bus . . ."

Adam nodded slowly. "You're right. We would have thought you were crazy."

"And now?" Sarah asked.

Adam looked up at the stone hearth and shook his head. "Who knows what to think?"

Sarah glanced back at the windows. It was still raining and foggy outside, but it was definitely growing lighter.

"But you still want to leave, don't you?" she asked.

"Yes. I was just waiting for it to get a little lighter, then I was going to wake you."

Suddenly, Sarah had a thought. "Instead of walking back up the road, can we find a boat and go across the lake?"

"Why?" Adam asked.

"Because there are houses on the other side," Sarah said.

"How do you know?"

"I've seen them," Sarah said.

Adam frowned. "When? I thought you said you've never been here before."

"I saw them in my dreams," Sarah said. "But

just like everything else I've dreamed, I know they're real."

"But everything you've dreamed happened in the sixties," Adam said.

"I know," Sarah said. "But I think it's worth the risk. I don't think we'll ever find our way out of here on the roads."

Adam stared at her, then pressed his fingers against his eyes and nodded. "I can't believe I'm agreeing to this."

They woke Jodie and went back to their rooms to get their packs. Then they went outside into the rain and fog. Sarah found the trail to the lake as if she'd walked it a hundred times. It was the strangest sensation, almost like stepping into a dream. They followed the trail to the green wooden landing that led down the cliff to the dock.

At the landing at the top of the steps, Adam stopped and leaned over the railing, looking down at the rocky shore below.

"Must be fifty or sixty feet straight down," he said.

"Don't say it," Jodie said, holding the wet rail tightly. "You know I hate heights."

"Hey, don't—" Adam started to say.

Suddenly Sarah heard a cracking sound. The railing Adam was leaning against began to give way.

"Adam!" Jodie screamed.

Trying to regain his balance, Adam reached out. Sarah grabbed his hand and yanked him back onto the landing.

"Wow, thanks," Adam gasped. He looked pale. "I guess this wood's pretty old and rotten. We'd better be careful going down."

"You lead the way," Jodie said.

They started carefully down the steps. A slowly drifting mist crossed the lake, making it impossible to see the other side. Adam glanced back at Sarah and gave her a worried look, but she didn't know how to respond with Jodie there. Adam would just have to trust her. She *knew* there were houses on the other side of the lake.

They reached the bottom of the steps and walked out onto the dock. There were two catamarans floating in the water beside the dock, and half a dozen Jet Skis. The surface of the lake was smooth.

"Anyone know how to sail?" Sarah asked.

Adam and Jodie shook their heads.

"There's probably not enough wind anyway," Adam said. "You guys ever used a Jet Ski?"

"I have," Jodie said.

"Not me," said Sarah.

"It's not so hard," Adam said. "It's just a twist grip. You turn it, and you start to go. You let go, and the Jet Ski stops."

"What if you fall off?" Sarah asked.

"There's a safety cord you tie around your wrist," Adam said. "It shuts the ski down immediately."

"Well, I guess I don't have much of a choice," Sarah said, staring down at the Jet Skis floating in the water.

"Look at it this way," Adam said. "We'll get to the other side of the lake a lot faster this way than by sailing."

"What about our packs?" Jodie asked.

"I guess we'll have to leave them here," Adam said. "Once we get help, we can always come back and get them later."

He started to take off his pack, and the girls did the same. Sarah watched as he helped Jodie climb down off the dock and onto the first Jet Ski.

"Ooh, the water's freezing," Jodie gasped as she stuck her fingers into the lake.

"As long as you stay on the Jet Ski and don't do anything fancy, you really shouldn't have to get wet," Adam told her.

Jodie pushed the starter button, and the Jet Ski coughed to life and puttered. When she turned the twist grip, the ski whined like a lawn mower and began to go forward.

"Just wait for us," Adam shouted over the noise of the engine. "You don't want to get lost out there in the fog."

As soon as Jodie had maneuvered the Jet Ski a little way from the dock, Adam helped Sarah climb down and straddle her Jet Ski. It felt like being on top of a skinny but wobbly horse.

"Just try to keep your balance and you'll be

okay," Adam said, as he attached the safety cord around her wrist.

"Tell me again. How do I make it go?" Sarah asked.

"Turn the grip toward you," Adam said. "Always do it slowly. If you turn it too fast, the Jet Ski will jump, and you could fall off."

He started the Jet Ski. Sarah tried the twist grip, and heard the engine beneath her start to whine as the Jet Ski moved forward on the water.

"Turning it away makes it slow down," Adam said. "Got that?"

Sarah nodded.

"Oh, no," Jodie said.

They both looked at her, floating on her Jet Ski about twenty feet from the dock.

"Mine just stalled," she said.

"Okay, I'll be there in a second," Adam said, climbing down onto his ski and starting it.

A moment later he pulled up next to Sarah, who'd been giving her ski little bits of gas and then backing off as she tried to get used to it.

"Got the feel of it?"

"I hope so," Sarah said.

"Just remember, always give it gas slowly and release the gas slowly," Adam said. "Now, I'd better go start Jodie's again."

Adam steered his Jet Ski away. Sarah turned the grip, and heard the engine of her Jet Ski start to whine. She started to move through the water.

Suddenly, without warning, the grip began to twist further toward her. The engine roared loudly, and the Jet Ski kicked forward.

"Too much gas!" she heard Adam shout behind her. "Ease up!"

Sarah tried to turn the twist grip away, but instead, the grip continued to turn toward her, as if someone else was turning it.

"I can't!" she cried. "Something's wrong!"

The Jet Ski was picking up speed. Sarah looked over her shoulder and saw that Jodie and Adam were disappearing in the fog behind her.

# Chapter 28

Sarah's Jet Ski was still picking up speed as it splashed along the smooth surface of the lake. She held on, trying to twist the speed control back down, but it seemed as if an invisible hand was keeping it at full throttle.

Sarah didn't have time to wonder whose invisible hand it was. She was too busy holding on for dear life while she tried to figure out how to stop the thing.

Then she remembered the safety cord.

She yanked on it.

The engine sputtered and died. The Jet Ski immediately began to slow down.

The next thing Sarah knew, she was floating quietly on the still water, surrounded by a veil of fog. In the distance she could hear the whine of the other Jet Skis.

"Sarah!" It was Adam calling for her.

"Sarah!" It was Jodie.

Sarah was just about to shout back when she heard something that sent a chill down her spine. Someone shouted, "Here! I'm over here!"

It was her voice, her words.

But it wasn't her.

Adam sat on his Jet Ski, letting it idle and listening for Sarah's voice. "Where?" he called.

"Here! I'm over here!"

The voice was coming from his right. Adam steered in that direction. He blamed himself for letting Sarah get lost. He shouldn't have expected her to know how to use a Jet Ski, based on a few simple directions. The other dumb thing he'd done was to race after her, leaving Jodie behind.

Now they were all separated.

He stopped again.

"Sarah?"

"Here, over here!" She was still over to his right, and she sounded scared.

Adam was just about to start moving again when he heard another voice call, "Adam!"

It was Jodie, also lost somewhere out there in the fog.

"Over here, Jodie!" Adam shouted. He heard an engine rev up, but it sounded like it was moving away from him, not toward him.

Jodie was just about to go in the direction of

Adam's voice when she thought she caught a glimpse of red hair through the mist. If she could team up with Sarah, the two of them together could try to find Adam. She gunned the engine of her Jet Ski.

As she got closer she could see Sarah bent forward over the Jet Ski, floating still in the water.

A second later Jodie pulled up beside her.

"You okay?" she gasped.

Sarah nodded, her red hair obscuring her face.

"Okay, look," Jodie said. "You have to remember what Adam said. If you start to go too fast, just turn the twist grip away, and it will slow the Jet Ski down."

Jodie placed her hand on Sarah's to show her how it was done. But Sarah's hand felt cold and clammy.

"Huh?" Jodie pulled her hand away. At the same moment, Sarah turned to face her. The ends of the safety cord were wrapped around Sarah's hands.

Before she knew what was happening, Sarah had looped the cord over her neck.

"Hey, what're you doing?" Jodie tried to pull the cord away.

Sarah yanked the cord tight. *Die! Leave Adam to me!* The cord started to choke Jodie. Jodie's hands went to her neck, and she tried to wedge her fingers under the cord. But Sarah pulled the cord tighter.

"Stop!" Jodie wheezed, her mouth agape, gasping for air that would never reach her lungs.

Sarah squeezed the cord tighter. Jodie hit her on the shoulders and side of her head, but it didn't matter.

It took another few moments. Then there was a splash as Jodie's lifeless body toppled over into the water.

# Chapter 29

Jodie was floating facedown in the water, the safety cord pulled tight around her neck. Sarah sat on her Jet Ski, staring at the body. Two distinct voices were speaking in her head. One asked: Why had she killed Jodie? The other said: Finally, it was done. Now she'd have Adam all to herself. Which voice was hers?

"Sarah?"

Sarah looked up. Floating on his Jet Ski in the mist forty feet away was Adam. They stared at each other.

"What's wrong?" Adam asked. "Where's Jodie?"

Sarah pointed at the body floating in the water.

Adam's gaze dropped, and Sarah saw the shock of recognition in his eyes.

Adam gasped. "You . . . you killed her," he said in a trembling voice.

"No," Sarah said.

"Yes, and Matt, too," Adam said.

"No."

"You did, Sarah. Why?"

"I didn't," Sarah said.

She heard Adam rev his Jet Ski. Sarah stared down at Jodie's body floating in the water. Was it possible she *had* killed her? Out of the corner of her eyes, she saw the mood ring on her finger. It was yellow. Why wasn't it black? Suddenly Sarah thought she understood what was happening. She looked up just as Adam turned away.

"Stop!" she cried, feeling the twist grip turn in her hand, and her Jet Ski kick forward, following Adam.

The two Jet Skis raced through the fog. Over the roar of her own Jet Ski, Sarah couldn't hear Adam's, but she could follow the wake his Jet Ski left in the water. She had to catch Adam. She had to explain what was going on before it was too late.

Before anyone else was killed. . . .

Sarah leaned forward on the Jet Ski, her hand twisting the speed control as far as it would go, her eyes glued to the foaming white waves of Adam's wake.

Suddenly she realized the mist was lifting. Ahead she could just make out the dock they'd left behind earlier. Adam was heading right for it.

A few moments later Adam pulled up next to the dock. In his haste to climb off the Jet Ski and onto the dock, he fell, painfully twisting his ankle.

Rising to his feet, he began to hobble along the planks toward the stairs that led up the cliff.

Sarah arrived at the dock, climbed up onto it, and started to chase him.

"Please, Adam, wait!" she cried.

Halfway down the dock, Adam turned and looked back at her with terrified eyes, but kept going.

Sarah sprinted after him. Now Adam had reached the steps and begun to climb them. Sarah ran as hard as she'd ever run in any race. She reached the bottom of the steps before Adam had reached the top of the first set of stairs.

"Wait!" Sarah cried. "You have to listen!"

Adam kept climbing, frantically pulling himself up with his arms to take the weight off his hurt ankle. The steps cut back and forth up the face of the cliff like a fire escape. On each set of stairs Sarah felt like she was gaining a step on him.

"You have to stop!" Sarah cried.

"No!" Adam yelled back. He was panting heavily. "Go away! Leave me alone!"

They were almost two thirds of the way up the cliff. Sarah was at Adam's heels. She could hear him gasping for breath.

"You have to listen," she shouted. "If you don't, who knows what will happen!"

"I know what will happen," Adam called back. "You'll kill me, too."

"No, no, I swear I won't!"

By the time they reached the last set of stairs, Adam was so tired and in so much pain, he could barely take another step. He clung to the rail, pulling himself forward. Sarah was right behind him, and not nearly as tired.

Finally Adam reached the landing at the top of the stairs. He tried to stagger a few steps toward the trail back to the inn. A split second later Sarah reached the landing. With a burst of energy, she flung herself forward and tackled Adam around the legs.

"Ahhhh!" Adam grabbed his ankle. Sarah tried to wrestle him to the ground, but he knocked her away. He hobbled a few steps, but she could see that he couldn't put any weight on his bad ankle. A moment later he tumbled to the ground.

"Leave me alone!" he cried.

"You have to listen to me," Sarah said.

"No!" Adam crawled backward, trying to escape.

"I'm not going to hurt you," Sarah promised.

"Why did you kill Jodie and Matt?" Adam gasped.

"I didn't," Sarah said. "But I think I know who did."

"You're lying," Adam gasped. "I saw you with Jodie."

"But I didn't kill her, I swear. You have to listen," she pleaded.

Adam kept crawling toward the woods, watching her over his shoulder as he dragged his injured foot. Sarah stepped toward him. She reached down and grabbed his hurt ankle.

"Ow! Ow!" Adam writhed in pain. "Let go! Let go!"

"Only if you promise not to crawl away," Sarah said.

"Okay, okay! Just let go!"

Sarah let go of his ankle. Adam leaned against a tree trunk and stared at her. She could see the fear in his eyes.

"If you didn't kill Jodie and Matt, who did?" he asked, breathing hard.

"Listen," Sarah said. "Remember when you thought you saw me running through the woods?"

"I didn't just think I saw you," Adam said angrily. "I *know* I saw you."

"How do you know?" Sarah asked.

"Because it was you," Adam said. "It was your body. It was your hair."

"Did you see my face?" Sarah asked.

"No, but what difference does it make?" Adam asked. "How many people have bright-red curly hair? We're the only people around, Sarah. Who else could it be?"

"I think there *is* someone else around here who looks like me," Sarah said. "You and I saw her on the television."

"When there was no electricity in the inn," Adam said.

Sarah nodded. "I know it sounds crazy. A lot of

crazy things happen around here. And one of them is that this person who looks like me is going around killing people and trying to make everyone think I did it. She gets in my thoughts somehow and makes me think crazy things. I swear, she's trying to make me think I'm the killer."

Adam gave her a mistrustful look. "Who is she?"

Suddenly Sarah saw something out of the corner of her eye. She stared in disbelief as her heart filled with terror and dread. She raised a shaking finger and pointed toward the beginning of the trail.

"Her," Sarah said.

# Chapter 30

"She looks just like you. . . ." Adam's gasp was barely more than a hoarse whisper as he struggled to stand up beside Sarah.

Sarah nodded. The girl standing with her hand behind her back at the edge of the trail had Sarah's face and Sarah's hair.

"But see her clothes?" Sarah said. The girl was wearing an old pair of bell-bottoms and a denim work shirt. And she was wearing beads around her neck.

"They're from the sixties," Adam said. "Like the girl on the television last night."

"Your name's Sharon, isn't it," Sarah said to the girl.

The girl nodded.

"How did you know that?" Adam asked.

"I've had dreams," Sarah said. "She's in them."

"Hey, Sharon," Adam said. "Why don't you talk?"

Sharon said nothing. She just stared at them.

"What does she want?" Adam whispered.

Sarah looked back at Sharon, who was no more than thirty feet away. "You killed Mike, Doug, and Ellen, didn't you?"

Sharon nodded.

"Who are you talking about?" Adam whispered.

"Remember the television," Sarah whispered back. "We watched her being arrested." She turned back to Sharon. "You killed Mike and Ellen because you wanted Doug for yourself. Then when Doug rejected you, you killed him, too."

Again Sharon nodded.

"This is getting crazier by the second," Adam whispered hoarsely. "What's going on?"

"Sharon and Mike were boyfriend and girlfriend," Sarah explained quickly, never taking her eyes off Sharon. "But Sharon liked Doug, who was with Ellen."

"So she just killed Ellen and Mike?" Adam asked, amazed.

"I'm pretty sure," Sarah said with a shrug.

"But what's all this got to do with us?" Adam asked. "I mean, are you saying Sharon killed Matt and Jodie?"

"Yes," Sarah said.

"But why?"

Sarah turned and looked into his handsome blue

eyes. They were racked with fear and bewilderment. "I think it has something to do with you and me."

"You and me? What are you talking about?"

Sarah took a deep breath. "The night before we left on this trip, what happened after we met at the mall . . ."

"So? I told you it didn't mean anything."

"Not to you," Sarah said. "But it triggered something in me. I can't explain how, but it must have brought her back. Ever since then, I haven't been myself. You said so yourself."

But Adam was no longer looking at her. Instead he was staring past her at Sharon. Sarah turned and saw why—Sharon had taken a step toward them.

"I don't like this," Adam said. "She looks really creepy. Maybe we should get out of here."

"It won't work," Sarah said.

"How do you know?"

"We'll never be able to get away from her," Sarah said, turning back to Sharon. "What do you want?"

Sharon took another step toward them and pointed at Adam.

"Me?" Adam gasped.

"Why?" Sarah asked. "Because he rejected me, the way Doug rejected you?"

Sharon nodded and came closer. Now she was only fifteen feet away.

"Sarah . . ." Adam hissed, terrified.

"It's not the same," Sarah said.

But it was as if Sharon didn't hear her. She was coming closer. Now her hand started to come out from behind her back, and Sarah saw something metallic.

"The knife!" Adam gasped. Sharon was still coming toward them. Sarah slipped her arms around Adam and helped him limp back onto the wooden landing at the top of the stairs. Sarah noticed that sunlight was glinting off the lake. For the first time in days, the clouds were breaking up, and the sun was coming out.

"What are we going to do?" Adam whispered desperately.

"Keep talking," Sarah whispered back, then turned to Sharon. "Killing won't help."

For the first time, Sharon spoke. "Yes, it will."

"No," Sarah said. "He isn't Doug. This isn't the sixties. You're not even alive."

"He hurt us," Sharon said ominously.

"Us?" Adam said. "What's she talking about?"

"Sharon and I are connected," Sarah said. "Remember the date of her execution? It was the day I was born."

"You're . . . you're the same person?" Adam gasped.

"I'm not sure," Sarah said.

"But you don't want to kill me," Adam said.

"No, Adam," Sarah said. "I admit I was jealous of you and Jodie. I wanted you for myself.

But I'd never kill for that. Never."

"Yes, you would," Sharon said. She was only ten feet away now. Sarah's heart was pounding and her breaths were short and fast.

"Look," Adam shouted angrily at Sharon. "Just get out of here, okay? Just go away!"

An evil smile appeared on Sharon's lips. The knife seemed to glow in the sunlight. She stepped closer. Sarah and Adam had backed toward the railing of the landing above the stairs. With Adam's bad ankle, Sarah knew there was no way to get down the stairs. She let go of Adam and stepped in front of him, placing herself between Adam and Sharon.

"Don't kill him," she said.

"You want me to," Sharon replied.

"No, I don't," Sarah said. "I want him to live. Even if he doesn't want me."

Sharon came closer. It didn't look like anything could stop her.

"Jeez, why did I ever have to kiss you?" Adam groaned behind Sarah.

Sarah turned and looked surprised. "Because you wanted to. You were curious. Didn't you like me at all?"

"I guess." Adam shrugged. "I don't know. It just happened. I mean, if I'd known this was going to happen . . ."

Sharon smiled and took another step closer, raising the knife over her head. "See? He never liked you. He just used you."

Sarah and Adam backed against the railing.

"No," Sarah said. "It was my fault too."

Sharon was only a few feet away. The knife was high in the air, its blade catching the sun. "Get out of the way."

"No." Sarah refused to move from her place in front of Adam.

Sharon was within striking distance now. Adam and Sarah pressed back against the rail. "Move away!"

"No," Sarah said. She reached behind and felt for Adam's arms, wrapping them around her. She could feel his body pressing against hers. It was exactly what she'd wished for. . . .

"Move!" Sharon shouted, holding the knife in front of Sarah's face.

Sarah felt herself tremble as she looked up at the razor-sharp blade, but she didn't move.

"Move!" Sharon screamed.

Sarah felt Adam squeeze her more tightly. It was all she ever wanted. If only it could be this way forever!

Sharon waved the knife, but didn't bring it down.

"You can't do it," Sarah said. "You can't kill me, because you'd be killing yourself. And I'll never move out of the way to let you kill Adam."

Sharon's movements seemed to slow down and stop.

Sarah held on to Adam's arms, keeping them wrapped tightly around her. "I'm sorry," she whispered to him. "I really am. I love you, but I never meant to hurt you."

"It's okay," Adam whispered back. Sarah felt him squeeze her back.

The knife fell to the floor of the landing and clattered against the wood. Sharon stepped toward Sarah. She was becoming filmy, almost translucent.

"What's happening?" Adam whispered.

"She's disappearing," Sarah whispered back.

Sharon took another step. Now she was almost nose to nose with Sarah, but she was just a vague image, hardly more than a shadow.

"You wouldn't hurt someone you truly loved," Sarah whispered.

Now hardly more than a silhouette, Sharon stepped forward and seemed to enter Sarah.

Sarah felt a cold chill race through her body. Sharon took another step. . . .

And disappeared inside her.

Then the railing Sarah and Adam were leaning against snapped.

# Chapter 31

Somehow Sarah managed to cling by her fingertips to the edge of the landing floor. Below her she heard Adam's sickening scream and then an awful thud. She looked down and saw Adam's body sprawled on the rocky shore.

How? She wanted to cry. How could it happen now? She felt weak with anger, pain, and frustration. After all the effort and energy she'd expended, she didn't think she had the strength to pull herself back up.

"*Let go,*" a voice inside her whispered. "*Let go.*"

It was Sharon's voice, her voice.

Maybe she should just let go.

Maybe it no longer mattered. She'd lost everyone. Her parents hardly cared about her, anyway. What did she have to go back to? How could she live with herself, knowing what had happened was partly her fault?

Yes. It was better if she let go.

Suddenly she felt hands slide around her wrists. With a gasp, she looked up into Sebastian's face.

"Let go!" she pleaded. "Let me fall!"

"No."

She hung helpless as he slowly pulled her back onto the landing. Then he put his arm around her waist and led her back up the trail toward the inn. She walked in shock, too shaken and stunned to cry, feeling almost totally numb. So much death. She couldn't feel anymore.

"I'm sorry about your friends," Sebastian said.

She looked up into his gray eyes, amazed. "You know?"

Sebastian nodded.

"Where have you been?" Sarah asked.

"Here," he said.

"All along?"

"Yes."

"Why didn't you do something?" Sarah cried. "Why didn't you help us?"

"That's not what happens here," Sebastian said.

"Here?" Sarah looked around. "What happens here?"

"Things," Sebastian said.

"What about Sharon?" Sarah asked. "How long has she been here?"

"Long, long time," Sebastian said.

"And what about me?" Sarah gasped.

"Now you're here too," Sebastian replied. Then he took her by the hand and led her back . . . to the New Arcadia.

## About the Author

T. S. Rue is a pseudonym for an award-winning writer of novels and novelizations for teenagers. Among his best-known works are *Home Alone*, *Friends Till the End*, *The Diving Bell*, *Beyond the Reef*, *The Accident*, and *The Mall from Outer Space*.

When he's not writing, Mr. Rue is usually on the road, speaking at middle schools, junior highs, and conferences. He likes to fish, play tennis, and spend time with his wife and two children.